MALICE

GUARDIAN SECURITY SHADOW WORLD
BOOK TWELVE

KRIS MICHAELS

CHAPTER 1

alice stared down at the small huddle of buildings lining the frozen-ass, iced-over coastline of the Buor-Khaya Gulf in Siberia. The locals referred to the town as Nayba.

He preferred to think of it as Hell.

Arctic winds moaned in a ghoulish cacophony as they pushed off the harsh, jagged plates of ice jutting up in mangled angles along the seashore and raced south across the Siberian tundra. Ice crystals pelted any exposed skin with knife-sharp edges. Frostbite happened within minutes. The cold was a bitter fucker, a ruthless assassin, and it was relentless. His gear was the best money could buy, and still, the cold would kill him if he let down his guard. He gave a sneer of respect behind his facemask and goggles. That he understood, and that was the reason he was able to survive in the harsh and unforgiving landscape. The tundra was covered in snow many meters thick. His camouflaged exterior layers kept his location hidden. The fur and high-tech layers he wore under the outer shell kept him alive.

Malice moved slightly to focus on the building where his target resided. He had a limited amount of almost dawning light to recon the small village. This far north, daylight didn't happen at this time of year, and the faint yellowing of the horizon was as much light as he would get. The scope he used filtered and amplified the existing light. He caught movement from one of the buildings and focused on the person moving in the bitter cold. The village had electricity, which he would take out when he was ready to strike his target. The stacked cords of wood would keep them warm until the generator was repaired. Maybe.

He rolled onto his back and stared at the gray blanket of clouds that dipped low and rolled with wind gusts. The faint light of day would wane soon, and then he'd enter the village. He'd find and kill Feliks Rostova, the head of the Rostova Group, a Russian state-funded private military organization. By his count, there were twenty-seven people in the village. Seven were non-combatants and lived in two small structures far east of the other fortified buildings.

It was time for his final mental preparation. He visualized the route to his target for the thousandth time. The way in was obvious; the plan, not so much. Malice reached over and put his hand on the backpack he'd take with him into the village. The contents were scaled down from his other pack, but they would keep him alive as he made his exit from this godforsaken land. But that would be after he killed the bastard he was sent to eliminate.

He would move silently and rig the outer buildings to blow simultaneously as he entered the main structure. If he calculated the charges correctly, there wouldn't be any need to worry about aid coming from behind him. The explosions would be his edge. He had that unexpected moment to enter and kill as many as possible with his fully automatic assault weapon. The target would fall by a bullet, or he'd gut the fucker. It didn't matter to him how it happened. The men who followed the bastard would defend him, and so they were also coded targets. He was there for

Rostova, but he'd take out every last person who blocked that goal.

Mal rolled over again and lifted his scope to make sure his pathway was clear. Fifteen paces from building one to building two. Twenty-one or twenty-two paces from building two to the main structure. He'd visualized the route and formulated a time hack. The detonators currently in his pack were set. He only needed to affix the bombs to the structures and start the countdown. The plan was solid. What wasn't was his accounting of the twenty bogies. In the time he'd been watching the village, the Arctic had taken a dump on that portion of the world and driven everyone inside. He hadn't had an accurate accounting of who was where in two days. But he couldn't wait any longer. His stores of goods were finite, and his extraction point was set. The time of extraction was still fluid. After finishing this mission, he'd travel one hundred and fifteen kilometers north and east to the administrative city of Tiksi before making contact and requesting extraction.

He stared through his scope. An itchy feeling under his skin crawled restlessly, and he listened to that feeling. It had saved his bacon on more than one occasion. Something was off. Something he couldn't quite put his finger on was out of place. Malice searched the village. What was it? What couldn't he see?

A low, haunting moan of wind accented the feeling that something was wrong. Malice expanded his search from the village outward. Drifts of snow, some thirty feet in height, had formed outside the village, starting at the rocky shores and building as record amounts of snow fell on the empty land. He glanced at the sky. The twinge of light proving it was, in fact, daytime had receded, and the dancing bands of the aurora borealis twisted in a green hue of modulating particles. He would never understand the natural beauty that could be found in the most austere conditions. But then again, maybe because the environment was so uninviting was why such splendid phenomena still happened. Humans hadn't fucked it up … yet.

His watch vibrated under the high-tech gloves and liners he was wearing, and Malice moved to his knees. He slung on his pack and held his snow-camouflaged, insulated rifle in his grip as he approached the village.

Anya Baranov laid silently as she watched through her scope. She kept her rifle trained on the area where she'd thought she saw movement. She heard her spotter's clumsy climb up the ice to where she watched the landscape around her.

"The assassin is not coming," Dima said, plunking down beside her. She ignored him and focused on the white image of snow she could see through the scope. Dima sighed loudly. "I did not have any choice."

Anya's eyes narrowed. That was a lie. She'd heard the conversation. "Liar." Her anger at Dima and the position he'd placed her in wouldn't distract her from her mission. She knew the plan and would follow through with it, regardless of the cost of life.

"You should be honored. Karl is Colonel Rostova's oldest son. He will inherit everything." Dima tried again.

"You promised we would stay together." Not that she wanted to be with Dima; he was a pig, but he also liked men, so sex wasn't a concern.

"Officers take field wives all the time."

Anya was tired of this conversation. "Fuck you, Dima." She snorted. The Rostova Group. It was supposed to be elite. *Elite*. Maybe so. They had food and boots without holes, which was more than she could say for the frightened little boys at the current war's bloodied edge.

As a sniper team, she and Dima were lauded. As a woman within the military, she was considered a whore. As a sniper, she was a valuable commodity on the open market. When she left the military, her spotter, Dima Agapov, and she sold their services to the highest bidder. She and Dima were paired together in the military, and the acquaintance had become comfortable. So much so that she discovered Dima was not interested in females, which made her feel safe. A sensation that was hard to acquire in the Russian military. So, when they both left the service, she stuck with Dima when he told her they had a job offer. That offer was from the Rostova Group. Since most of the men in the Group were recruited from special forces, the sexual disdain they held for women was the same as in the military.

Dima claimed her as his field wife to protect her, which kept the others away from her. A field wife cooked, cleaned, and gave sexual favors to the officer who claimed her. It was a common occurrence in the Russian military. Dima was an ass, but she knew him. Yet, with her skill as a bargaining chip, he'd advanced in the ranks within Rostova's cadre. She was his property, or so all the men in the camp believed. It didn't matter at first. But then, as Dima rose, she started to see what the Rostova Group was doing. Where her skills were used. She wanted nothing to do with some of the missions, but alas, she was in too deep. Walking away wasn't an option. She had no money, no transportation, and no hope of a distraction big enough to cover her exit. Anya had learned to become as invisible as possible, and she watched everything. One day, she'd find a way out.

As the only woman in the camp except for the Indigenous people who lived on the outskirts of Nayba, she stayed out of sight and out of everyone's way. Unfortunately, her efforts were for naught. She again thought of that night as she scanned the snow-covered horizon, looking for the movement she'd seen earlier. She hadn't imagined it.

Anya slipped silently into the empty kitchen of the main building. It was late, and she assumed everyone was asleep. She was wrong. Hearing boots come down the hallway, Anya ducked into the kitchen's pantry and prayed no one would see her. She'd seen the leers and had heard the comments. She wasn't a valenok. Idiots didn't live long, and she planned on living as long as her babushka.

"Coffee." Colonel Rostova's command was sharp and loud. Chairs around the kitchen table scratched against the wood floor. Anya carefully moved away from the floor-length curtain that separated the pantry from the kitchen.

"Where is the dispatch?" Colonel Rostova barked out the question.

Anya could hear coffee being poured and papers ruffling. "Here." That was Karl, Colonel Rostova's son. A shiver of absolute terror, fear, and revulsion ran down her spine. Rostova's son was an evil man. She carefully inched farther away from the curtain. No one in the camp scared her except Karl. The things she'd witnessed ... She shivered again—the pig.

"So, this is good. We have received payment from Abrasha Molchalin. We can bring up the recruits from Africa and advance the men we already have."

"Switzerland will not know what hit them." She didn't recognize the person who said that.

"Our forces will have the correct passports?" Colonel Rostova asked.

Karl spoke, "Yes. The initial force will go in through the established checkpoints. We will take them all out at the same time after our people are in place. Then, *our reinforcements will drive across the border, bringing our arms and ammunition. I will leave in the morning to make sure all is in order. Fifty thousand men is a huge undertaking and not an easy task to conceal, but we have a good plan. The initial force will be small but deadly. The rest will come in when we need them."*

"The banks will be the first target?" Colonel Rostova asked.

"Yes. We will control the physical structures and computer system access. That will give Abrasha Molchalin what he wanted, correct?" Karl asked.

"His people will be ready to take over the banking computer systems," Colonel Rostova acknowledged. "We take the country, and the Russian leadership must acknowledge our power. Abrasha will pay us one-third of the money he obtains. The Kremlin will acknowledge us, or they will fall."

There was silence followed by a sudden round of laughter. Anya could only imagine the obscene gesture that was made.

"What about this bullshit?" Karl's voice broke through the laughter.

Colonel Rostova's response stilled the laughter. "Yes. This information came directly from the source. An assassin has been deployed to remove me."

There was scoffing at the table, and she heard Dima ask, "Who would dare come here?"

Anya crossed her arms. The bastard had kissed Rostova's ass enough to be included in planning?

"We paid a great amount of money for this. An American from this organization is coming. Guardian," Colonel Rostova said. "We will be ready and waiting for him. Dima, take your woman to the overwatch. Pavel and Ivan, my most trusted lieutenants, will rotate duty in front of this building. No one comes in or out without my permission. Kill anyone you do not recognize."

"When do you want us posted?" one of the men asked.

"Get sleep tonight. It will take time for the assassin to travel here."

"This information is five days old," Karl said. "Are you sure you want to take that chance?"

"Do not count your old man out, Karl. I will sleep with two guns instead of one tonight." Colonel Rostova laughed. "Go find your beds."

The meeting broke up, but Anya held completely still. She could stuff her coat with bread, cheese, and dried meat, then head out before the men took up position in front of the house. Anya reeled at the information. This could be her way out. Maybe she could use this assassin as a way out. But how?

"*Dima, a minute,*" *Colonel Rostova's voice called out.*

"*Yes? I am at your service,*" *Dima said.*

Anya rolled her eyes. He was such a cocksucker.

"*Your shooter. My son wants her.*"

"*Sir?*" *Dima cleared his throat.*

"*Do not worry. You will still work with her, but she will be his field wife when you are not on duty. We will make it worth your inconvenience; you will be handsomely rewarded.*"

"*When?*" *Dima asked.*

"*When I get back from organizing things for the Switzerland invasion,*" *Karl said.* "*Have you used her?*"

Dima was silent for a moment. "*I have not.*"

"*Why?*" *Colonel Rostova asked. There was silence for a long time. How in the hell was Dima going to get out of this one?*

"*I am not so inclined,*" *Dima said. Anya's eyes popped wide. Dima admitting he preferred men was dangerous. Very dangerous.*

Karl laughed, and she heard someone get slapped on the back. "*Father, I will leave Dima in your capable hands as I believe you both have the same inclination. Dima, make sure she understands I will make good use of her, and she will comply, or she will be beaten.*"

"*I will,*" *Dima acknowledged.*

She heard Karl leave. "Dima, you took a chance admitting what you did," Colonel Rostova said. "You will never admit it again. It could be a death sentence for you."

Anya narrowed her eyes. But not for Rostova? Interesting.

"I understand, sir," Dima admitted.

"Then it is not just my son who has found a new field wife, is it?"

"No, sir." Dima sounded scared, and Anya was happy he was. He should be. But she wasn't worried about his future. She was more concerned about hers. Her life was being decided for her, and that was something she couldn't allow. She'd had enough. Once she heard them leave, Anya let out a long, silent breath of air. She turned to the shelves and started to fill her pockets. The assassin was her ticket out of this hell. But how could she escape? What would he do? How would he attack? How could she leave? Would there be an opportunity? And most importantly, how long would Karl be gone?

Focusing back on her scope, Anya caught sight of the man as he lurched to his feet. She watched as he made his way to the small collective of buildings.

"He is not coming. It's too cold to be out here."

"Then go warm Rostova's bed," Anya said as she watched the assassin. The man was damn good. Never giving her a solid target. She could hit him but not take him out.

"Say that again, and you will be punished," Dima hissed.

She snorted. "I can say what I want." Dima had given up any right to be included in her plan for the future.

"What are you looking at?"

"A rabbit," she said, looking up at him. It was the first time she'd looked at him all day. "What happened to you?" He had a black eye and a split lip.

"Nothing." Dima shrugged and looked away. Anya doubted that. A lesson from his new husband, perhaps?

She dropped back down to her scope. It took almost a minute before she found the assassin. She shifted. "How many meters to Pavel's pit?"

"I told you three hundred twenty-seven," Dima said.

"Wind?"

"Why? Do you have a target?"

"Wind!" she demanded. Dima grabbed the handheld device.

"From the north at fifteen kilometers an hour. What do you see?"

She watched the man as he darted from one building to the other. Pavel lifted in his pit. By setting her ballistic drop compensator, Anya had already calculated for the cold and gravity. She adjusted for the wind and squeezed the trigger.

MALICE SANK beside the first structure, shrugged off his pack, and pressed the charge of explosives against the back of the building near a fenced area of propane containers. He hit the timer and stepped off with the second charge and his weapon. He paced off the distance, affixed the charge, then stepped off again.

Malice froze when the snap of a bullet sang past his ear. He dropped to the ground when a man, positioned in what appeared to be a pit, fell forward out of the snowy area onto the ground. The report of the weapon snapped again. Mal lunged forward. Stopping was not an option. He'd be blown to hell. Malice sprinted toward the main building. Another report of that high-powered rifle cracked through the eerie cold-enforced silence of the permanent nighttime, but the bullets didn't hit near him.

Just as he reached the stairs, the buildings behind him blew. He slammed himself against the side of the target's building and waited. The door sprang open, and men flew out of the building. Malice pulled the trigger on his assault rifle and yet was still able to hear the percussive twang of the sniper's gun singing. Men to his left fell as he fired to his right. His plan had been shot to shit. The unknown sniper was laying down suppressive fire from the south. Malice spent his magazine and reloaded before he rolled around the corner of the door and into the target's building.

He lifted his weapon and fired. The three-bullet burst took out the first and second man in the hall in front of him. The third dipped into a room off the hall, and Malice sent another burst of five-point-five-six caliber ammunition through the wood paneling. He moved forward and kicked in the door where the man had disappeared. Dead. Malice shifted sharply and walked silently down the hall, attuned to the building's silence.

Approaching the corner, he kept his weapon trained and, with his non-firing hand, reached down and snapped a hand grenade from his belt. A quick slide of his thumb eliminated the pin. He counted, tossed the grenade into the area around the corner, and took cover. A scurry and scream preceded the explosion.

Mal was up instantly and rounded the corner. He found several targets, but none of them were moving. He moved through the room to a heavy wooden desk that the grenade had turned into toothpicks. He cleared the side of the desk in sharp movements, then focused behind it.

His target sat against the wall. A piece of the desk about a foot long and a foot wide had embedded itself in the guy's intestines. Blood dripped from his ears, nose, and mouth, but the bastard was still alive.

"Why were you sent to me?" the man asked in Russian.

"The world doesn't want you in it," Malice replied in English.

"American filth." The man coughed up blood. Malice kept his weapon trained on the man and swept the area again.

"Mouthy for a dead man." Malice brought his attention back to his target.

"Leave me. I am, as you say, dead," the man said, even as he choked on his blood.

Malice placed the barrel of his weapon on the temple of the man's head. He looked at the man and shook his head. "No." He spoke the single word before pulling the trigger and splattering gray matter, hair, and skull against the dark paneling.

Malice moved out of the room and sprinted out of the building seconds later. There was no gunfire as he moved. He made his way back to his pack and grabbed it at a dead run. He sprinted to the maze of drifts he'd followed into the village. As soon as he had sufficient cover, he stopped, secured his six, and reloaded his weapon. Assessing the situation, there was only one course of action to take.

He needed to find the sniper who had saved his ass and determine what the actual fuck was going on. He was a one-man mission. If another agency was working on that clusterfuck, it would've been nice to know.

CHAPTER 2

*A*nya Baranov hissed as she pushed herself back into the insulated tent she and Dima had shared until a few minutes ago.

She slid the tent's zipper down and started the small heater that warmed the confined area. Inside, she opened the small medical kit they'd been provided when she and Dima had joined Rostova's elite forces.

With care, she peeled out of the layers of clothing that had saved her life. The knife Dima had shoved in her upper chest as they struggled for her handgun had hit home, but not to a depth that could kill her. She winced at the slice that extended from her collarbone to the top of her breast. She shook out a piece of cloth from the medical kit before tearing an alcohol pad free of its wrapping. She tore the pad in half, wiping the wound with the first part, then cleaning the needle, which she would use to sew her flesh together.

Threading the needle was hard. She was shaking. Not from the cold. Her small tent was hidden, obscured from sight, and almost warm. It was the adrenaline that made her shake. When she'd fired the shot to take out Pavel hiding in the pit in the camp, Dima had freaked. She lifted the handgun she'd hidden under her tarp and fired. The small caliber bullet hadn't stopped the bull of a man. He was on her before she could pull the trigger again. When he lifted to plunge his knife into her, she fired again and pushed him off her. Anya scrambled back to her firing position and cleared the path for the assassin. After all, it was her shot that had alerted the forces in the camp of his arrival. She watched until the assassin entered the building, then moved. He was on his own from that point forward. Rolling Dima off her tarp, Anya folded it quickly and shoved it into her pack.

The seven point six two caliber brass casings of her rounds were picked up, and she scanned the area for anything other than Dima's body that would show she was ever present. There was nothing. She carefully retraced Dima's footsteps, obscuring her own, and moved as quickly as possible to the tent she'd erected two nights earlier. It would take a skilled tracker to find her, not that it would matter soon. When Rostova didn't check in, forces would be sent to ensure their leader's welfare. Depending on the weather, she had twenty-four hours, maybe a bit more, before Rostova's people would flock to the area. Yet the time spent sewing herself up was necessary.

With the thread finally through the eye of the needle, she pinched her cut together and pushed the needle through her skin, piercing the left and right sides in one motion. She'd stitched up many cuts. It sucked. The pain was more mental than physical for her. The anticipation of the needle piercing the skin made her muscles shake, which made her job of knitting the two folds of skin together much harder. She dabbed at the blood that oozed from the cut as she worked.

"North," she said to herself with her teeth clenched around the thread she was holding tight while her finger pushed the needle again through her flesh. "One hundred kilometers. Easy."

Anya worked and talked to herself. It was an old habit; one her babushka had instilled in her. Her father's mother lived until she was over a hundred years old and survived wars, political exile, the death of children and grandchildren, and the cold of Siberia. Her babushka said talking to herself broke the monotony of isolation and kept her from going insane. "I do not doubt it," Anya said in conclusion to that thought. She knotted the thread and let the remainder of the thread and needle dangle from her teeth. She freed her knife and sliced the thread. With the alcohol pad, she dabbed at the blood. The stitches would hold, and she would heal.

Anya cleaned up her supplies and stored the bloodied pads in a resealable plastic bag that would hide the odor from animals in the area. She used a clean alcohol pad to dab away at the blood clotted around the reindeer fur she wore next to her skin. The alcohol would dry quickly. Pushing over to sit next to the heater, she rethread the needle. The necessity of repairing the sliced material was a matter of life or death. The cold was her biggest danger, and having holes in her layers could cost her life. She stitched quickly. Each minute that passed was a minute she could be farther away from the tiny village and the onslaught of Rosto-va's men.

It took another thirty minutes to make sure her clothing was sufficient for the journey ahead. Anya put her pack together and made sure there was enough room for the small tent and portable heater. The battery was nearly gone, but the tent would provide shelter from the wind, and she could survive with the clothing she had. It would be miserable, but when had life not been that way?

Anya turned off the heater and removed the silicone bones that held the tent up. She let the tent top rest on her head as she packed away the heater, broke down the bone structures, and put them in her pack. She put on her gloves, made sure every-thing was put away neatly, grabbed her rifle, and unzipped the front of her tent.

She flipped the flap back to exit. The barrel of an assault rifle two inches from her face stilled her immediately.

"Why did you take out your own men?" The American's Russian was good. Anya sat back on her butt and looked up. Her seal coat's hood dropped back, exposing her ushanka, a fur-lined felt hat with earflaps tied under her chin. The American's eyes narrowed slightly. That was the only reaction to her being a female. "Many reasons. We must go. Rostova's people will be coming."

The gun didn't move. "Not good enough," he said in English.

Anya replied in English, "I did not want to be sold and used like a whore. When I found out you were coming, I decided to help you kill the people who would buy me." She snarled at him, "Self-preservation is a strong motivator."

She couldn't see the face behind the cold-weather mask, but she could see his eyes through his goggles. "Your spotter?" he demanded.

"The one who was doing the selling." Again, she urged the assassin to move. "Rostova's people will come when he does not check in with his men."

"You don't work for any other agency?"

"No. I worked for Rostova until you came."

"You said they knew I was coming?"

"Yes, that is why the men were waiting for you in camp. If he shot you, my plan to escape would be …" She searched for the word and muttered it in Russian.

"Fucked up," the man supplied.

"Yes, this," she agreed.

"How much notice did you get?" The American's question was quick and to the point.

"Three days." She moved to the side so the gun's muzzle wasn't focused on her forehead. "Three days for me. I was hiding and overheard many things." She shook her head. "Rostova's son said the message was five days old." Anya sighed. "If you are going to kill me, please do so. Otherwise, I must go. I do not want to be found and used."

"We'll move." The American slung his gun over his shoulder and took her rifle from her. "I'll carry this and the handgun." He extended his hand.

Anya looked up at him. He lifted his eyebrow behind the winter mask. She pulled the ancient weapon out, grip first, and handed it to him. He glanced at it, then at her. "Do you have more ammo?"

"No." She had one bullet left in the revolver. It was the one her teacher had always told her to reserve for herself. No one wanted to die at the hands of the enemy.

He flicked open the barrel, spun the chamber, and closed the weapon. The handgun would have to be fired twice before the bullet advanced to the chamber. He handed it back to her.

"Sure of yourself. Americans." She put the

weapon back in the holster she'd made from reindeer hide.

"The same could be said of Russians." He watched her break down her tent and start to fold it. His hand landed on her shoulder. "You're injured?"

Anya glanced down at a drop of blood that had frozen dark red, not brown, and was obviously fresh. She looked up at him. "I am still able to leave this place."

"That wasn't what I asked."

"That is what I answered." Anya finished folding the material and shoved it into her pack. She swung it on, hissing a bit when the pack pulled her shoulders back.

"We'll go north," the man said.

Anya looked up at him. "North. Yes. There is food and resources."

The man didn't say anything as he moved forward. She hitched her pack into a more comfortable position, covered her face and neck with her fur-lined scarf with holes cut out for her eyes, and started after him.

His pace was quick but not exhaustive. She used his tracks when possible to avoid tiring herself more. Soon, they found a small thicket of coastal reeds that formed a concave in the snow and went back a distance. The man moved back into the wind-hollowed recess. She waited. If a lynx or wolverine was willing to fight for its territory, she'd let the American deal with it. He appeared at the mouth of the depression and motioned for her to follow.

Anya glanced back at their trail. The American was smart. He'd kept to the low ground, where tracks between drifts would be covered almost immediately and their travel wouldn't be as visible. She glanced at the sky—the ominous clouds boiled above her. The concave would do well in the weather bearing down on them.

She walked back along the ice-covered path. There was an ice shelf formed around the reeds. The man stood looking at the clouds. "There's another storm coming," the American said before dropping his backpack and pulling out what she thought would become a shelter. He assembled the structure in seconds. The rods popped into place, and the material stretched tight. He pulled out another piece of white camouflaged material and snapped it over the top and the sides of the structure. He opened the flap and placed his backpack inside the small hut. "I need to debrief you."

Anya let her pack slide off her shoulders and hit the ground. "What is this? Debrief?" She didn't like the sound of it, whatever it was.

"My superiors will want to know what you know." The American stopped what he was doing. "Do you have supplies?"

"I have some food. My heater is old, and the battery is almost gone. My shelter, you saw."

The man nodded. "Let's get into the shelter, and then we'll talk."

Anya hesitated. She didn't know the assassin. "I can build my shelter."

The man stood and straightened. "If I were going to hurt or take advantage of you, I would have done so at gunpoint. Unless directed, I don't kill women or children. You're a bit of both. You have information my superiors will need. Like it or not, according to you, we will soon be hunted, and to get out of this mess, we'll need to work together."

"I am twenty-seven." She stood to her full height.

"Good to know," the man said before disappearing inside the structure.

Anya dropped her head back and looked at the sky. Snow blew sideways, building against the shelter. Within an hour, the back of the tent would be insulated from the wind by a wall of snow. The American knew what he was doing. She grabbed her pack and moved into the cramped space.

A small plastic stick hung from the top of the tent, illuminating the interior of the shelter with a yellow glow. He had already started taking off his cold-weather gear, and she scanned him. His dark hair stood in all directions. His beard was almost black, except for a few stray gray hairs. He was attractive, rugged, and not unlike some of the people she'd seen in movies. Handsome in a way that drew a person's eye. Well, at least her eyes.

She moved to the corner to watch as he worked. He pulled out a large metal tube and unscrewed the top. "Water." He poured some into the lid and handed it to her, taking a swig out of the bottle as he held it out. She accepted the cup, removed her scarf from in front of her face, and upended the cup. He set the tube beside her and started pulling out small silver packets, which unfolded into sheets. Anya watched with great interest. He wove the sheets into the posts of the shelter, then moved as he spread two under him. He handed her two packets, and she followed his lead.

"Foil emergency blankets will insulate us and keep it warm," he said as he took off his parka and sat on it. She pushed her hood back and took off her ushanka. Her blonde hair fell to her shoulders. She moved a bit, easing the pull on her stitches. She was in pain, but it was better than being dead.

The American pulled out a small black box and opened it. He pushed a button and looked at his watch. "We have thirty minutes before my superiors make contact."

Anya glanced at the box, then at the American. "What is it you want to know?"

alice stared at the wide, deep blue eyes of the woman in his tent. Her blonde hair and pale skin made her seem otherworldly. He took another drink of water and filled the cup for her. He'd boil and filter another container after he spoke with Guardian. Reaching inside his pack, he pulled out two high-calorie protein bars and handed one to her. "What's your name?"

As the woman shifted to take the bar, she couldn't hide the wince of pain. She was in obvious discomfort. He didn't know how badly she was injured, but based on her ability to keep up with him on the march, she should be okay.

"Anya Baranov. What is yours?"

"Mal." He didn't give a last name. The young man who had a last name didn't exist anymore. His alias was used for buying property and investments.

The woman unwrapped the bar and took a bite. Her eyes closed, and she chewed slowly, savoring the food as if she hadn't eaten in a while. "Mal? Is this a name?"

"It's short for Malice," he supplied. "What did you hear the night you learned I was coming?"

Anya finished chewing her food and looked at him. Those dark blue eyes were intelligent, and he sensed the woman had been through a hell of a lot in her twenty-seven years. Something he recognized in her look echoed back at him. "Malice like anger, yes?"

"That's right," he said and waited while she took a drink.

"It was three nights ago. I was getting food at the main house. I do not eat with the men. I stay out of sight. When I was there, I heard things. Dima was going to hand me over to Karl Rostova when he returned. Perhaps for money, perhaps not. I do not know."

"What? Explain that."

Anya sighed and pulled the foil down on her

bar. There were spots of blood on her fingers and under her nails. Her fingers were long and slender, and since she was the sniper who had pulled the trigger saving his ass, they were strong and capable, too. "In the Russian military, women are … less. When we are sent to units, officers claim some as field wives."

What in the hell? "Field wives?"

She nodded. "We cook, clean, and other things." Those blue eyes lifted and met his. "Dima was not interested in me, but he claimed me because I am …" She seemed to search for the word she was looking for and then said sharpshooter in Russian.

"A sniper," he provided the English word for her.

"Yes," she agreed. "He made money and position from my skill."

"Why would he give you to someone, then?"

"He was now in Rostova's inner circle. Anyone who is brought here is. The most trusted. This is a stronghold."

"But not you?"

"No. I am a woman. I am less. Dima was at the table the night Colonel Rostova told his lieutenants you were coming. Women are not less. We should not be less."

Mal heard the despair in her voice, but he couldn't focus on that. He needed information. "Can you tell me exactly what was said?" Malice needed the precise words.

"Yes. They had just finished talking about the war in Switzerland."

Malice's head reared back. "There isn't a war in Switzerland."

"There will be."

The woman took another bite of her bar. Malice waited for her to swallow before he spoke. "Explain that."

"Abrasha Molchalin, he is oligarch. You know this word, yes?"

Malice nodded. "I do. Continue."

"He paid Rostova for fifty thousand men. They are gathering to enter Switzerland. Not all at once. But Karl Rostova has a plan."

"When and why?"

"I do not know the when except soon. The why they talked about. The banks." Anya shrugged. "Rostova would claim the victory. Molchalin seizes the banks and assets. Something about computers and money."

"Russia wants Switzerland?"

"I do not know if Russia does. Rostova does."

She cocked her head. "The Westerners would be pulled into the fight, yes?" She stopped with the bar halfway to her mouth. "Is this right? Would Americans fight for Switzerland?"

"Probably." Malice nodded. *Fuck*. What in the hell had he stumbled on? "What else was said?"

"Talk of moving resources closer to Switzerland. Rostova's son, Karl, is in charge of this. He left with the snow machines three days ago."

"And of my presence?"

"Yes." The woman nodded. "Rostova said the …" Anya stopped. "The …" she groaned and said the word in Russian.

"Information," Malice provided for her.

"Yes. It was reliable and came from computers to the organization sending you. Guardian, yes?"

Malice narrowed his eyes. "What else was said?"

She looked up and to her right, thinking. That action alone lent credence to her story. Liars usually looked down and to the left. "He paid for direct access to the information." She glanced back at him. "He put Dima and me on overwatch. Pavel and Ivan took turns in the interior snowbank waiting for you. I had days to plan my actions and escape. You were late."

"The storm." Malice shrugged.

The woman nodded and took the last bite of her bar. "This was good." Malice handed her his; he hadn't even opened it. "No." She shook her head. "I will not take from another."

"You aren't." He pulled a mesh bag out of his backpack, revealing a trove of high-calorie bars and pouches filled with food. "Eat."

She took it from him and peeled the foil away from the bar. "Your superiors, will they take me out of Russia?" Anya didn't lift her eyes when she asked him. It was almost as if she expected him to say no.

"I'll ask." She'd saved his ass and given them a fuckton of information. Hopefully, they could validate what she said.

She stared at her bar, not moving. "It would be good to not be here." The words were said quietly, almost like a prayer.

"How long have you been here? In Siberia?"

"I grew up near here. About six hundred kilometers to the west. My babushka's family came from the gulags. She raised me. When she died, I joined the military."

"Your mother and father?"

"The winter is hard on people." Anya shrugged.

"Do you have a family?"

"I do, but they're not blood. People I trust with my life." Malice pulled out a bar and opened it. He took a bite, and Anya smiled at him. There was a slight gap between her front teeth that was cute as hell. Malice blinked at that thought. He'd been away from people for too long.

A beep sounded from the box next to him. Malice opened the box, pulled out the earpiece, and inserted it.

"Authenticate Hate." The connection was poor, but he could hear Fury's words.

"Power. Secure, plus one."

"Explain." The word snapped through the crackling connection. Malice wasted no time in relaying he'd completed his mission and included the fact that he was expected and that Anya had provided cover fire. He then related what she'd overheard about Switzerland.

"CCS, take over. I have to up-channel this information ASAP," Fury spat out.

A new voice said, "You're sure they said it was through our systems?" It was the female CCS lead who asked the question. She was a constant in his reporting process.

"As it was relayed to me, they had direct access to the information."

"Fuck." The woman sighed.

"Exactly," Mal agreed. "I need extraction for two."

"I copy," a man replied. He didn't recognize the voice, but as long as they were on the connection, they had to be authorized. He was probably one of her assistants. "Threats in the area?" the man asked.

"When Rostova doesn't check in, we will be hunted." He looked at Anya, and she nodded.

"Can you get to Tiksi?" the woman asked.

"Yes, but not while Rostova's group is hunting us. We're safe now, but if they have any heat-sensing equipment, we're dead." Malice knew what the odds were. So did the woman beside him. She shrugged as if saying she didn't know if they had the equipment.

"Can you fortify your location and keep under the snow? That should limit their ability to pick up your signature."

"There's snow and ice everywhere. We can get under it if we need to."

"I copy. Supplies?" the male voice asked.

"Enough for two weeks if we're cautious."

"Be cautious," the woman said. "There's a storm coming off the ocean, and it's basically a hurricane. It'll be a bitch." The connection crackled loudly. "There's no way any aircraft could get to you. If you tried to get to the extraction point, you'd be in whiteout conditions. The weather system is massive. Hunker down, and we'll notify you when we have this worked out."

"I copy."

"CCS is clear."

As Malice pulled his earpiece out, Anya bent closer. "A phone in your ear."

"Satellite communications. Yes." He held out the device in the palm of his hand.

She stared at it but didn't move to touch it. "What did they say?"

"A bad storm is coming in off the sea. They want us to stay put and wait out the storm, then hide from Rostova's people when they arrive."

Anya leaned back and stared at him. "Hiding this close to Nayba is not a good plan."

"I agree." Malice didn't like it one bit.

"We move north when the storm lessens. There are people …" She said a series of Russian words.

"Indigenous people," he supplied for her.

Anya nodded. "Yes, they are travelers and move

with the reindeer herd. We can get food and supplies from them if we need them. Trade, yes? We can move during the storm if we are smart. Staying is not smart."

Malice agreed, but then again, moving now wasn't an option. Now, they needed water and to hunker down. "I'll get snow to melt for water." He reached for the clothes he'd taken off.

"I can do this. I need to visit nature," Anya said.

Malice dug out the pot and small cook stove from his pack. He handed her the pot. "For snow, not nature."

Anya tossed back her head and laughed. "I am not a valenok," she said before bundling up and moving out of the shelter.

He smiled at her Russian word for a simpleton. No, he had no doubt she was as far from a valenok as she could be. There was immense intelligence in those eyes. He was dressed seconds later and out of the tent. He held his assault weapon at the ready with the safety off. Did he trust her? No. But then again, trust was built, not given. He thought about the old revolver he'd given back to her. The thirty-eight caliber was a big enough bullet to delay and maybe piss someone off unless the bullet went through the brain.

Finding her hadn't been easy. He initially headed in the direction the bullets had come from, coming up with a rough trajectory. Then he started looking for places a sniper would use to set up. He moved quickly and was lucky when he'd seen the place she'd struggled with her spotter. A smooth depression with a deep hole. He recognized the hole for what it was. A footprint. Then he moved toward the camp, and that was when he found the shooter's location. He knelt and read the information left at the scene. The first shot hadn't taken the bastard out. The bloody knife was under the spotter's body. Malice had studied the area carefully. The wind obscured part of the story, but from what he could see, she'd shot the spotter, struggled with him, and he'd tried to stab her. The woman had guts, and that earned her some respect.

He'd tracked her back to her shelter. She was damn good at covering her tracks, but he'd been taught by the best. The fact that she was a woman had taken him by surprise. Working with Val, it shouldn't have. He watched the snow swirl above him, the wind buffeted by the high drift of snow and ice. She turned the corner, a full bucket of snow in her hand and her revolver in the other.

Anya trudged up to him. "Have you ever peed on an arctic fox?" She had to shout the words.

Malice burst out laughing. "Really?"

The woman waved the handgun toward the path. "He was not happy." Malice watched as she opened the shelter and ducked in. He had an idea his time with the woman would not be boring.

CHAPTER 4

*J*ewell pulled her hands through her hair and screamed.

"Feel better?" Zane asked from the doorway.

"No."

"Warn a person next time." Con's voice came over the speaker. "I about had a fucking heart attack."

"Sorry," Jewell said to both of them. "What are we missing? How did they know Mal was coming?"

"Did they know Mal was coming or just someone?" Zane asked as he came up behind her. His hands went to her shoulders, and he started to massage the tight knots that had formed.

"Mal said they had direct computer access and knew it was a Guardian. That's all I know." Jewell shook her head. "I know for a freaking fact we've defended against the NSA's invisible worm program."

"Yeah, we're golden. Jonas reverse-engineered that program to protect his systems, and we copied his efforts plus made improvements," Con agreed. "What are we missing?"

"What about Honor's program?" Zane asked.

Jewell turned to look at her husband. "What?"

"She's the only other one who's burrowed past your firewalls. We know Dean Benedict sold the program Honor created," Zane noted.

"No, she told me how to subvert that. My programs would have activated." Jewell shook her head. She'd had nightmares about both of those damn programs and was positive she'd guarded against them.

"What if it was modified?" Con's voice over the speaker was cautious. "Think about it. Jonas was brilliant, and we're only a third of the way through the data we recovered from when Ice called us into his mission. The man was a freak, but he was a demented genius. What if he changed the program?"

"But there isn't a centralized hub anymore. We blew it up. If the program is listening or gathering data, how would it get to Rostova's people?" Jewell grabbed a pencil and shoved it between her teeth for a second before tossing it across the room. "Direct computer access." She shook her head. "Direct computer access. That has to be the key. Who has access to our information about the movements of our shadows?"

"The Mountain, the Rose and the Annex, and us, of course," Con said. "But logistics … Travel could be the weak link … Did he fly commercial?"

"No," Zane said. "Military transport to Alaska, then CIA trawler to Russian waters. He was taken in by trusted indigenous allies. From there, he walked to his target."

"None of the logistic entities knew anything about the other. There's no way he was tracked via travel." Jewell sighed. "Direct computer access." That had to be the key. It *had* to be.

"Then it's a Guardian feeding the information to someone," Con said the words Jewell had been dreading.

"*Who*? No, I won't believe that. Anyone with the clearance to know about coded missions has been vetted a thousand times." Jewell shook her head and stared at the screen.

Zane cleared his throat. "If it wasn't us, it could have come from someone on the Council. Why would Jonas target our systems that are so strongly defended when he could pluck low-hanging fruit?"

Jewell turned slowly to look at her husband. The Council consisted of nations that had bonded together to go after the worst of the worst. They worked in secrecy, no one knew who sat on the Council except the members, and it was a lifetime appointment. Death was the only way off the membership roles, and it was a finite membership.

"Oh, fuck." She hadn't even thought about a system outside of Guardian.

Zane nodded. "I'll get ahold of Archangel." Zane moved into the communications room.

"Con …" Jewell's hands flew to her keyboard.

"I'm on it. We're going to need access to those systems to run the patches and see if one of the Council members has been compromised. We can't give them the program. It can't be allowed to propagate. It has to be contained."

"I know. I'll make sure Jason knows. I'm remoting into the mainframe system at the head-quarters mountain."

"I've got all our programs up." Con was moving as fast as she was.

"Right, me, too. We're green, all green." Jewell worked furiously.

"Nothing. We haven't been compromised, Jewell. That standalone computer that Archangel talks to the Council on hasn't been accessed. Guardian is safe. It wasn't us."

"How many systems will we need to access?" she said almost to herself.

"I don't know." Con sighed. "We're in uncharted waters."

Jewell stared at her screen. "But how would the Council members know *when* Malice would show? That isn't given out to the Council. Only that the target is coded."

"A logical assumption would be that the mission would happen sooner rather than later, right? But how did they know a *Guardian* asset would be coming?" Con worked through the problem with her.

"I know. The organization to perform the mission is assigned at random via an algorithm, so no agency has more chance than the others of being tagged for the missions." She tapped her fingers on the desk beside her keyboard. "We're

47

missing something."

"Who controls the randomizer?" Con asked.

Jewell drew her bottom lip into her mouth and bit down on it. "The chairman of the Council."

"That's where we need to start," Con said, and Jewell nodded, even though he couldn't see her.

"Agreed. They knew it was a Guardian. We start there."

"Babe, I have Jason online," Zane called from the next room.

"Con, I'll be back." She popped out her earpiece and sprinted to the secure communications room beside her systems.

Jewell slid into the chair in front of the camera that would show her to Jason. "Jason, we've got a major issue."

"What is it?" Jason took off his glasses and stared at her.

"The target knew a Guardian was coming."

"Yes, I am aware. Joseph told me."

Jewell held up her hands, stopping her brother. "No, wait, you don't understand. Con and I think we've figured out *how* they knew." Jewell leaned forward closer to the camera. Zane's hand landed on her shoulder, and she sat back down in her chair. "The chairman's computer."

Jason's head snapped back. "Excuse me?"

Jewell's hands flew in a rapid-fire motion in front of her body, trying to settle herself down enough to say the words so everyone understood. "We know for a fact we weren't hacked. We're protected. We've made sure of it. I don't know who the chairman is, but the target knew a *Guardian* was coming. The only way that information could get out is if Jonas accessed the chairman's computer system. From the chairman's computer, you could obtain the target and the agency assigned. Nothing else. Not who else was on the Council, only that the target was coded and the entity who was selected to go after the target."

"How would he know who the chairman is?"

"Jason, I don't know, but I'm certain whoever the chairman is, he's been compromised. You have to get me or Con to that system. We can protect them. All of them, but we aren't releasing the patch to the world. They can blindfold me and take me to where I need to go. I don't need to see anything but a computer screen." Jewell stood up and started pacing. "You have to get us access."

"Jewell."

"I can let them watch. One of their system's people, but they can't have the code. I'll have to put a stone wall around it, so they can't try to break into what I'm doing and figure things out."

"Jewell."

"Then we can monitor the systems like we do yours. Not the communications, just the security." She turned and walked the other way. "Will they trust us to do that?"

"Jewell!" Jason's thunderous roar stopped her.

"What?" she yelled back.

"I'll call you back when I have permission." Jason's image was gone a second later.

"Well, that was rude." She looked at Zane. He opened his mouth, then shut it again.

"Wasn't it?" she asked.

"Let's get that system patch ready. We'll work through what just happened here after that."

Jewell frowned. "Was I rude?"

"No, babe. I'd say driven." Zane stood up. "Remember, Jason has more than this on his plate. He's probably overwhelmed, too."

Jewell looked at her husband and blinked. What else did her brother have on his plate?

Zane lifted his eyebrows. "Switzerland. World War Three?"

Jewell frowned at him. "What?"

"You didn't listen to anything about that call except what pertained to your systems, did you?"

She grabbed her husband's arm. "No! Was I supposed to?"

Zane pulled her in for a hug. "Nope. You're focusing on what you need to focus on." He released her, and Jewell stared at him. "Your brain is the most beautiful thing." He pushed her hair away from her face. "Now, go get that system update ready, and I'll get our go bags sorted."

She nodded and followed him into her computer room. Zane stopped by the mini fridge and pulled out a bag of tiny chocolate covered peanut butter cups and a soda. "You earned this." He put both beside her keyboard.

Jewell pulled the bag open and put her comm device back in her ear. "All right, Con, we need to prep for all possible computer languages. I don't know what operating systems the chairman's computer runs."

"Already ahead of you. I'll send you the languages I'm working on. You grab the others."

"Got it." Jewell pulled up the note and popped the top to her soda. She was going to need all the sugar she could get. It would be a long damn day.

CHAPTER 5

*A*nya stripped down, taking layers off as the tent got progressively warmer. The American, Mal, short for Malice, had done the same. "This is wonderful." She pointed at the thin silver blankets.

"Your wound. Do you need to tend to it?" Mal nodded to her chest.

Anya pulled out her shirt and glanced down at the stitches she'd sewn. They'd held but bled a little. Her skin was red and inflamed. That was to be expected. Her pack was heavy and pulled her shoulders back, stretching her skin and muscles. But none had ripped. "No. The sewing is holding."

"You closed yourself up?" Mal stopped sharpening the knife in his hand.

"Of course. Would you not?" She cocked her head.

Mal blinked as if her question shocked him. "I would."

"Then why would I not?" She shrugged. "Women are not less."

Mal put the knife back into its holder and stretched out on his side of the tent. "You keep saying that. Women in my country are respected and treated as equals." He stopped and then moved his head from side to side while rolling his eyes. The gesture was endearing, as was the expression on his face. He looked at her. "Correction. For the most part, women are respected as equals. There are some who would like to keep women subjugated as second-class citizens, but that's the minority, not the majority. America is far from perfect."

"Women in Russia, especially in the military, are not respected unless you have … *blat*."

"What's that? Blat?" the American asked.

She rolled onto her back and stared at the top of the shelter. "Ah, this is connections. It is the way things operate. Want a job? It is who you know. Want special privileges? Make a call to someone who knows someone else. You will owe, but that is the way of things."

"Ah, the good ol' boy network," Mal said as if her explanation made sense with those words. "We have that, too. But not in the military. There, it isn't allowed for either men or women."

"In Russia, this is allowed. Women in the military? It is not good. But I had nowhere else to go. When my babushka died, there was no reason to stay. I don't want to be less. I do not deserve to be less." Yet she couldn't help but feel that way at times. But not now. Not in front of this man. She changed the subject. "This Guardian, it is military, like Rostova, yes?"

"No. Guardian is private security."

Anya nodded. "Yes, like Rostova. Private security hired to fight wars."

Mal smiled and shook his head. "No. Private, not funded by the government. We are paid by the company."

"Yes, like Rostova. You are paid for killing people." Anya was trying to understand why the American was arguing with her. They were saying the same thing.

"No. Only a very few do what I do. We're called on when monsters need to be removed."

"Monsters." Anya cocked her head. "Rostova Group is this?"

"His military group was not the target. *He* was." The American laid back and supported his head with his arm. "He preyed on children. That's why he was removed."

Anya's mouth dropped open. Finally, someone saw what was happening. "Yes. For the young ones he and his son take from villages and send them to war for Russia."

"Yes," Mal acknowledged. "And for the ones in Africa his lieutenants use and kill in the mines and tunnels they're forced to work. And for those he sells." The American looked at her. "No one has the right to sell or give away another. *No one.*"

Anya stared at him for a moment. "In this, we agree." They were silent for a long time. The wind howled, but the structure stayed warm. Anya rolled on her side, adjusting her parka as a pillow.

"How long have you worked for Guardian?"

The man glanced at her. "Long enough."

She lifted her eyebrows but didn't say anything. Obviously, that topic was off-limits. "You were born in America?"

"Yes. In New York."

"Ah, the World Trade Centers." Anya shook her head. "War should not be waged on civilians."

"On that, we also agree," Malice said. "That's why my company protects those who can't protect themselves."

"Who pays for this?"

Malice shook his head. "I don't know. I've never asked."

"Huh." She would want to know, but Dima always said her nose would get her in trouble.

"It doesn't matter as long as the innocent are taken care of," the man added.

"Right," she agreed. "This, I understand. The concept is strange, though. Taking care of people who cannot pay."

"There are a lot of programs in the States that take care of people who don't have enough."

Anya jerked her head to look at the man. "Socialism?"

"No. Each person keeps what they earn, less the tax the government takes. We pay for our goods and services. The taxes pay for those programs."

Anya narrowed her eyes as she stared at him. "We say the same things, but you think it is different."

Malice chuckled. "It is different. Government assistance is not socialism."

Anya made a face at him. "If you say so."

Malice laughed long and hard. "You're going to be trouble, aren't you?"

Anya nodded. "Probably."

The American laughed again. "How did you learn to shoot?"

"Ah, in my hometown, there was one who was the best hunter. He had that." Anya nodded to her rifle. "When he saw me hunt, he worked with me. He had two boxes of shells for Nadia."

"Nadia? Your rifle's name is Nadia?"

"Yes." Anya nodded. *Was that not a thing in America?* "With her, we could shoot animals from a great distance. He showed me how to calculate gravity, wind, and distance. He said I was the best he had seen." She wasn't bragging. There was better than her, but not by much.

"Where did he get the rifle?" The American turned and looked at her.

"The war. He came home with it, and no one asked for it back. He was old, like babushka. When he died, I took the rifle." There little else of value in the old man's home. But she took care of his body and took the rifle and the remaining shells.

"Have you ever lived in a city?"

"Yes. When I was in the military, cities are dirty. Too many people. Rude people." Anya chuckled a bit. "Living out here, you respect nature, or it kills you. Living in the city will kill you."

Malice shrugged. "Some people don't know how to live outside the city limits."

"That is their loss." Anya sighed. The city and the military buildings were dirty and smelled of garbage all the time. She existed there but lived for the times they would leave the city. She blinked and jumped a bit. "Do you know Texas?"

"The state? I have been through Texas many times, yes."

"There are cowboys, yes?"

"Yes, there are cowboys." He chuckled.

"I watched a movie in the city. It had cowboys. The land in America is not much different from Russia."

"You're right. Except Siberia. Alaska is the closest we have to this place."

"A tiptoe across the ice," she whispered.

"What's that?"

"My babushka said if you ever want to escape

Russia, tiptoe across the ice to Alaska." She chuckled. "I thought of trying that many times, but I fear there is not enough ice in the world."

"Probably not, especially with global warming."

Anya frowned and looked over at him. "What?"

He waved his hand in the air. "A topic you don't want to get into, I promise."

Anya let that slide. She wanted to know everything about America. She'd never talked to an American before. "And Florida? Where the …" Anya made an ear with one of her hands. "Mouse."

"Yes, I've been to that amusement park once."

"Was it wonderful?" She'd heard one of the men in her old unit talking about the place. He was the son of a very affluent family, and he talked of the rides and food. The people who laughed and stood in lines for hours to see things she could only imagine. He showed pictures on his cell phone. She lingered over them and tried to memorize the scenes behind the people.

He turned to her, lying on his side so they were facing each other. "It was. It's a magical place."

"Maybe someday I will go to this place." Anya smiled at him. "In America, that is possible, yes?"

"Absolutely." The American smiled at her. "Have you been to Moscow?"

Anya shook her head. "No. I am from gulag family. I have nothing. I joined the military. I left. Dima convinced me to join Rostova. Now, maybe I leave Russia."

"We'll both leave Russia," the American said. "Where did you learn English?"

"My babushka. She taught English at university before she and my dedushka were sent to the gulag. He died before Khrushchev did away with most of the camps."

"Why were they sent to a prison camp?"

Anya shrugged. "Zvat' nikto, familiya—Nikak. *My name is nothing, my family name is nobody.* It is the truth of the gulag. There was no need for a reason. My family was sent. Then we stayed. Many did." They had a good life, though, especially with the conveniences of electricity and cell phones. Internet access was severely limited, and to access it, you needed a computer or a newer-style cell phone. Neither of which her family could afford, but she was enthralled with technology and had learned as much as she could in the military. Her world exploded in scope and size when she entered the military, and for that, she was glad.

"Do you have any family left here in Russia?" Mal asked after several long moments.

"No." She had no one.

"That will make leaving easier."

She sighed. "Maybe. This is what I know." She'd never thought about leaving Russia before meeting the man. Her dreams were smaller. A place that was warm, a man who loved her, and enough to live comfortably. Maybe a child. The Rostova Group was a poor decision on her part. One she would learn from.

"So, you will learn something new." The man closed his eyes. "We should sleep."

Anya stared at the man across from her. His dark hair and beard could not conceal his chiseled face. His skin was clear, and his teeth were straight and white. The bulk of his frame under his layers of clothes didn't protrude like an alcoholic's gut. His hands were clean, even under his fingernails. The clothes and equipment he had were far superior to hers. The earplug that was a cell phone was fantastical yet seemingly ordinary to this man. She closed her eyes. Perhaps she would be allowed to go to America. Perhaps not. The future held the answers, and one of her strongest talents was patience. She would wait and see.

$\mathcal{M}$alice waited until the woman's breathing settled and he was sure she was asleep. He pulled out his cell phone and tapped in a message.

> We are not safe at this location.
> Can you track this signal?

The responding text came back about a minute later.

> Now? Yes. The storm hasn't hit you yet.

Malice read Con's text.

> We will move north. I'll let you know when.

Fury?

Malice rolled his eyes. The ancient one wasn't on the ground, and he had no doubt the old assassin had ignored orders that didn't make sense when he was in the field. He'd bet last year's pay on it.

He knows I'll do what I need to do.
Status on info given?

Malice knew Guardian would disseminate the information about the pending attack on Switzerland, but the idea that someone had informed Rostova of Guardian's movements irritated him like a burr caught deep under his skin.

Not us. Working all.

The statement was less than he needed but was enough to alleviate the curling rage in the pit of his gut. He would track down the bastard who'd outed his mission and take them out if Guardian didn't do it first. If it hadn't been for Anya, he would have been a frozen piece of flesh in that compound.

Malice put the phone away and sighed quietly. If he didn't come back, his friends would mourn him, but no one else would miss him. His existence would flicker out, and the others would move forward with the lives they were building. Only he and Harbinger were without attachments.

He thought of Paris. She was a nice girl. He'd wanted to protect her and keep the world from hurting her again, but there was nothing sexual about it. Paris was too young, mentally and physically, to deal with someone with his baggage. He glanced across the tent. The illumination stick was waning, but he could see Anya. She said she was twenty-seven. He couldn't see it but had no doubt she was telling the truth. She was seven or so years older than Paris in age but a lifetime older in experience.

Life had dealt both of the women sucky hands. But in the game of life, you played what you were dealt, didn't you? Paris would make a good mom, and her sister, Londyn, and Ice would be there for her. That was the night and day difference between the women. Paris had support, medical care, a warm, safe place to call home, and a bright future.

Anya was a sniper and a talented one. She was smart and had figured out a way to save herself by saving him. The things she'd lived through and had to endure would break some of the men he'd known. The woman had his respect. She wasn't a wilting violet. Her dark blue eyes were something poems were written about. *Stop.* He rolled his eyes. *Where the hell had that come from?* He chuckled silently. It had to be the cold. *The stuff poems were written about.* He was losing it for sure.

Malice sighed, even as he thought about those eyes again. He'd seen some ladies in high society use contacts to make their eyes that deep sapphire blue, but there was nothing fake about Anya. If she'd ever worn makeup, he'd be surprised. She didn't need it. Her lips were red, and her eyes sparkled when she talked about America. She had a presence. No wonder Rostova's son wanted her.

He smiled into the darkening tent. Ice would have a field day with his thoughts. Damn, psycho psychiatrist. A smile formed as Mal thought about his friend. Hell, he loved the guy and was pleased he'd found his version of happiness. Londyn was good for him. Ice called him Mother Mal. Hell, all his friends did. Maybe he was a hair overprotective of his friends, but he'd always watched out for others. For as long as he could remember, he'd watched out for the young ones in the foster homes where he'd lived. The last house he was sent to before his eighteenth birthday had been a living hell. The "father figure" was a predator. The foster mother didn't believe him or the little ones when they told her that her boyfriend was a predator. She believed the pervert watched the children out of the kindness of his heart. Mal reported it to the social workers. The younger kids were terrified, but there was nothing the man could do to him. Or so he thought. A couple of the bastard's friends teamed up on him and beat him. He ended up in the hospital with his jaw wired shut. Mal swore then and there that he would get stronger and come back to hunt the fucker down.

He was sent to a group home after being released from the hospital. He took his GED and passed, then joined the Marines. Four years later, he returned and tried to find the son of a bitch, but his foster mother and her boyfriend were nowhere to be found. He got a job working for the police department, completed the academy, and worked hard at building a life. Until he responded to that incident.

Mal kept his shit together as his partner interviewed his one-time foster mother. She denied everything the child who'd reported the abuse claimed. Mal made sure to keep himself out of sight as much as possible. He talked with the social worker and the children, but he didn't engage with that bastard or the woman who had to know what was happening. No, he would come back and reintroduce himself.

Which was what he did one week later. He'd almost made it out of the house after ensuring the bastard would never sexually abuse another child. Almost. Two of the younger ones stood in the hall as he exited the bedroom. He'd talked to one of them the week before. Mal put his finger over his lips and motioned for them to go back to their room. The children did as they were told. Mal left the house.

Two months later, he was arrested for the murder of the bastard. A forensic interview of the child he'd interacted with that night had tied all the evidence together. The child identified him, and a damn good investigator pulled all the threads of Mal's past, including his report of abuse against the dead man, together and presented it to a grand jury.

Demos showed up two weeks before he was supposed to go on trial. Mal was expecting his court-appointed lawyer, but the man waiting for him was nothing like a lawyer.

"Sit down." Demos nodded to the chair across from him.

Mal sat down and stared at the man. "Who are you?"

"I'm called Demos. I'm here to offer you a proposition."

Mal leaned back. "You do realize I'm going on trial for murder in a couple of weeks. My ability to do anything for you is rather restrained at this point."

The man smiled. "Why did you kill him?" The suit-clad stranger held up a hand. "There are no recording devices here, and I haven't advised you of your rights. Nor am I an authorized law enforcement agent in this state. We're just having a conversation."

Mal cocked his head and looked at the man. "If I did kill someone, it was probably because he deserved it. People who prey on children deserve what destiny dishes out. Or so I'm told."

"Did you enjoy it?" The man lifted an eyebrow.

Malice stared at the man. Fuck it, he was going to go to prison for killing that bastard anyway, so he'd tell the truth. "I was taught how to kill by the military. Human life is fragile. It takes very little to end it. Enjoyment isn't a byproduct of my training, nor is guilt. Death is inevitable for everyone on this planet. No one is getting out alive, and some bastards deserve to go sooner rather than later."

A faint smile flickered across the man's face. "I can arrange it so you would be able to continue that type of work. You'd be able to take out the worst predators in the world."

Mal laughed. "Where do I sign up?"

Demos leaned in. "This isn't a game, nor is it a laughing matter. Make a careful and informed decision. You would work for an organization that demands complete loyalty. There are strict rules of engagement, and if you violate any of them, you will return to jail or be one of the ones gone sooner rather than later. This is a lifetime assignment. You will not get another chance to answer this question. Do you agree to live and perhaps die by these terms?"

"The people I'd ... take care of, they're all criminals?"

"The worst monsters in the world. You'd be trained to go after them."

"An assassin." Mal leaned back and stared at the man in front of him. He had nothing but prison in front of him. As a cop, he'd be a target inside. "I accept."

"This is what's going to happen. At two-thirty a.m., there will be a fire alarm activated at this facility. Your cell door will open. You will turn right. Go down the hall *and wait for the door to open. Make a left and follow the hall to the door. The door will release, and you will walk through it. Make a right and go out through the kitchen. A vehicle will be waiting for you. Get in. Make no deviations from this course. If you do, you forfeit your chance."*

"Right, left, right. I understand."

"I'll see you soon." The man stood and buttoned the suit coat of his incredibly expensive-looking jacket.

"May I ask who I'm going to be working for?" Mal stood, too.

"Ultimately, the oppressed and undefended people of the world. That's all you need to know for now."

Mal glanced over at Anya as she sighed and burrowed deeper under the blanket she'd pulled from her pack. The thing was old and thin but patched and clean. The woman took care of the items that would save her life. He'd scrutinized her rifle while he was leading them away from her last camp. The weapon was old but well-maintained. She'd policed her rounds, even when she was wounded, and she'd saved his life. Respect? Yeah, she had his respect, and he'd do whatever he could to get her out of that barren land that would rather kill you than host you.

Malice closed his eyes and suppressed a smile. The woman was unique and cute as hell. But that was something he didn't need to delve into. Cute could still be deadly. A woman with her talents was someone to be wary of, and he'd follow his gut. Yet, those eyes and that sass. Damn, the woman could be a major distraction if he let her be.

CHAPTER 7

*A*nya watched the American disassemble and stow the shelter. The wind was fierce, even in the protected area, but staying was not an option.

"Tie this to your waist," Mal said, handing her a length of nylon rope.

"Why?"

"Whiteout conditions are possible. I don't want you to get lost," he said, taking the other end and securing it around his waist. "Together, we have a chance of surviving. Alone, not so much."

Anya looked at the rope. "You mean, alone, I will perish."

Mal stopped what he was doing. "My equipment is better than yours. It isn't a reflection of your ability or mine."

Anya stared at him for a moment. "Then say that. I am not a valenok."

The American stared at her. She couldn't tell if he was smiling behind his mask and goggles, but she sensed he was. "I'm sorry. I will be more direct."

"Thank you." She tied the rope around her waist. "Compass?" she asked.

He pulled out a metal box and opened the device. They both turned toward the north and east. "Tiksi." He pointed.

"Before that are the travelers. We can trade for supplies."

"What would you trade?" he asked as they walked out of the sheltered area. The wind struck them with a force that made both of them lean toward it, bracing against the velocity. There was no way he would be able to hear anything she said. He glanced at his compass again, showed it to her so she could get her bearings, then pocketed it.

Walking was hard. Climbing the drifts that loomed in front of them even harder. They stopped to put on their crampons. The spikes helped them to get up the icy crust of the drifts. Anya's were of lesser quality, but she tied them on and kept up with him. They rested more than they traveled, but they moved away from the camp, which was the immediate goal. She admired the sense the American showed by traveling slowly and resting often. Most foreigners would try to move quickly. The sweat that formed on their skin would freeze, and their core temperature would plummet. The cold killed in more than one way in Siberia. There was no way a helicopter or a drone could fly in this wind. Land-based snow vehicles had limited range. The farther they moved away from Nayba, the better.

The faint rays of sunshine had long passed by the time they stopped for the evening. Anya took the pot they'd use to melt snow and filled it as he dug out a small area in the snow to protect them on three sides. Again, this man showed his knowledge of living in the extreme environment she'd grown up in.

She moved around the bank, found shelter from the wind, and made sure there was no arctic fox burrow under her before she took care of business. Men had it so easy, even with things like calls of nature. She moved slowly back to the shelter and stopped about ten feet away. A large paw print was almost covered with snow. Anya bent down and used her mitten to push away the fresh powder. A polar bear.

She lifted her head and looked around. They had been following the coastline, so it wasn't surprising to see tracks. Still, one swipe of that bear's claw, and the warm shelter Mal had set up would be gone.

She made her way back into the shelter. Another glowing stick hung from the center of the structure. It was good it wasn't too bright. Just enough to work and see each other. As soon as she took off her fur scarf, she spoke, "I saw tracks of a polar bear."

Mal looked up. "Then we cold camp again tonight." He put several pouches away and pulled out some more of the delicious bars. Yes, the American was smart. If that bear smelled any food, it would track them.

"Where did you learn how to live here?" Anya asked as she took one of the bars from him.

"Well, survival training, for one. I've been on several missions in the extreme cold. I'm a fast learner when my life depends on it."

"We all are, yes?" She watched as the snow

melted rapidly in the bucket she'd filled. Mal tipped the pot with the melted snow and poured it through a device that she assumed filtered the water. "I actually prefer the cold to the heat of the desert." He looked up at her. "Water in the desert isn't as readily available."

She agreed with him, although she'd never been to the desert. "How many places have you been?"

"Countries?" he asked as he continued to stream the water through the filter.

"Yes." She unwrapped her bar and took a bite.

"I never stopped to count." He lowered the pan and waited for the water to drip through. "Russia, the US, England, Scotland, Ireland, France, Germany, Portugal, Spain, Kenya, South Africa, South Korea, Thailand, Australia, New Zealand, Antarctica." He stopped and seemed to stare into space for a moment. "Peru, Chile, Venezuela, Switzerland, and Belgium. I believe that's it."

"Do you speak all the languages?"

Mal chuckled. "I speak Russian and French, and I've been known to slaughter the heck out of German. I believe I can talk to a two-year-old in Korean, but that theory hasn't been tested. Do you speak any other languages?"

"No. Just English and Russian." She took another bite of her bar. "The weather will get better soon."

"Yes." He poured more water into the filter. "We'll sleep for a few hours, then move on."

"This is a good idea," she agreed. "Karl, Rostova's son, will come back, I think."

"Instead of going on with the invasion of Switzerland?"

"He said prepare, not do. Besides, no one knows of this, right? So, why not delay the move on this country to gain revenge for the death of your father? I have met this man. He is …" Anya searched for the right words. How did she say he was dangerously overconfident? "He will follow in his father's steps. He will want to prove he is worthy to Putin and the rest. Finding out who killed his father would be first. Taking the country second. It is a matter of blat. He owes for his father's commitments after he has been avenged."

"Will he be one of the first to come back?" Mal asked as he poured her a large cup of water.

"I do not think so. Communications outages from storms happen. But once they find out, he will come back." She hoped the native inhabitants knew enough to leave the area. They only stayed to make money off Rostova's men by cooking and cleaning.

"Why did Rostova have Nayba as his stronghold?"

She snorted as she drank and then coughed. When she could talk, she cleared her throat. "Who in their right mind comes to Siberia in the middle of winter? Here is as safe as it gets." She shook her head. "When Rostova told of the assassin, everyone laughed. They could not believe it to be true. Even the colonel thought it was a joke. That is why only two were posted out. No one believed a person would be so bold."

"That mistake cost him his life." Malice opened his bar. "Also, if I were Rostova's son, I would come back, take my father's body to be buried, and set my men after the killers as I went on with the move that would now make *me*, not my father, great in the eyes of the country. I'd advance the timetable, not delay it."

Anya stared at the American long and hard. "You would do this?"

Malice blinked and looked up at her from where he was filtering more water. "Personally, no. But when tracking a target, one tends to get into the mind of them and any known associates, so you have an idea of what they might do. If the son has always been greedy, power hungry and ready to prove he's better than his father, he's a narcissist who probably would have killed his father if given the time. He expects the right to be in charge, even though he's done nothing to earn it. The psychological report done on him was very thorough. Also, the fact that Rostova didn't believe anyone would come after him was foreseen. He has a superiority complex, which isn't exactly a diagnosis, but it was as close as our doctors could get. Rostova proved his capability as the leader of this group. His hubris was well known."

"Hubris?" Anya could not place the word.

"Arrogance," Mal supplied.

"Yes. This was the word I was looking for. Arrogance." She took another bite of the bar and then stopped. She tipped her head and listened. "The wind has lessened."

Mal nodded. "We should finish and sleep. Then we'll move out. The more distance between us and Nayba, the better."

Anya agreed. Once she finished her bar, she helped him fill their water supply before they rested. She stared at his back and watched as his breathing regulated. Her eyes closed. He was a good man. Strong and smart. She prayed that, together, they would be smart enough to outthink Rostova's son. Tomorrow and the next day would tell.

alice woke suddenly and held still. What was that? He lifted his head, realizing he was spooning Anya. His body's reaction to her closeness was immediately apparent. He moved his hips and his stiff as fuck cock back a bit and blinked once or twice, orienting himself. Obviously, they'd sought each other's warmth as they slept. He looked down at her, and her eyes were open. "A motor," she whispered.

Malice sat up. The wind had died down. There. He heard it again. "Snow machines?"

"No. Listen. It is constant." She sat up, too. "Airplane."

Mal shook his head. "Helicopter." The whopping of the blades was discernible now.

"From the west," Anya said.

"They're traveling to Nayba," Malice agreed.

"They will know soon." Anya was up and putting together her pack.

Mal started to do the same. "We'll move quickly now that the weather's better."

Anya put her hand on his arm. "Quickly but not foolishly. Do not overheat."

Mal smiled and winked at her. "Let me know if I go too fast for you."

Anya snorted. "I will lead. You keep up with me."

Mal chuckled and made haste to break down the shelter after they geared up. The woman was a kick in the ass. They were heading north and east five minutes later. Anya took the lead and set a sustainable pace. They traveled for about three hours before he heard the sound of a motor again. He turned to see a light in the distance. The helicopter had a searchlight illuminated, and it scanned the ground underneath it. Shit. "Find cover," he said, and they both headed toward a drift about a hundred yards away. Malice dug furiously and pushed Anya in before him, covering her with his body and his digitalized snow camouflage, keeping the souls of his boots down so they wouldn't show as the helicopter flew by.

When he was sure the helicopter was gone, he moved off her. She backed out of the small hole. He brushed off the snow that had stuck to her hood and scarf. "How long before the son arrives?"

"I do not know where he is. We have a day. Maybe. Many men will come with him." Anya looked to the north. "We should not stop. We should move through and find shelter on the outskirts of Tiksi."

"I agree." It would be exhausting but necessary.

He pulled out the compass, and they oriented themselves again. The trek was arduous on a good day. Mal carried both weapons: his assault rifle and her sniper rifle. His pack was probably a good forty pounds. They rested often, drinking and eating to keep up their energy. The hours dragged by as they planted one foot in front of the other. There were no sounds except for the howling of the wind. Neither spoke. The gritty look of determination on Anya's face when she removed her fur scarf to eat or drink was probably etched in his expression, too.

By his reckoning, they had another fifteen kilometers to go. Anya sat on a piece of ice that jutted up along the shore. "Are you ready?"

She nodded and stood up, only to tip and stagger. He righted her and took her by the arm. "Are you all right?"

"Tired, but I can rest when we get there." She stood up and looked at his hand. He pulled out his compass, and they faced the direction they needed to go. Anya moved out. They passed the people Anya called travelers. The herd of reindeer was small, and if the travelers noticed the two strangers passing by, they gave no indication. Each time Anya stumbled, he steadied her. She was running on fumes, as was he, but he had better nutrition and conditioning on his side.

The lights of the small town were the most welcome sight he'd seen in years. "The shoreline. Look." Anya pointed to the darkened edges of the town.

"What are they?" The small square buildings did not have lights on.

"Potemkin village," Anya said as she started walking toward them.

"I don't understand what that's supposed to imply," Mal said as he moved after her.

She stumbled on the way down the hill, and he grabbed her arm, keeping her upright. "Potemkin villages are fake structures built by the lesser politicians to impress their bosses. This was done to impress the one in charge of this region. These look like houses from a distance. We can hide in one. Use your shelter inside, and no one will see us."

That sounded like heaven right now. As they walked toward the structures, the sound of snow machines roared to life. Malice grabbed Anya's arm, and they dropped down, squatting to make themselves less visible.

"Where?" she asked as she looked around.

He pointed. "There." At the edge of the town, lights bounced around as snow machines darted down the road out of the village. Three large tank-tracked trucks lumbered out after the slew of snow machines. The last one carried what Mal supposed was fuel by the shape of the container in the back.

"They go to Nayba. Rostova's son will be with them." She nodded to the convoy. "That is the truck he left in."

"And there's probably a contingent remaining here," Mal added. He helped her up, and they moved on to one of the buildings. It was, in fact, a plywood structure, basically a box with a roof. They squeezed through a warped area at the back of one. Anya dropped to the ground. Mal couldn't blame her. He found a level area and popped his shelter up. He draped the inside with the emergency blankets and pushed her pack inside. He helped her up and into the shelter. "Sleep."

When he zipped up the door, he went to work. With fishing line, he put up a warning system should anyone come close to the building they were occupying. The sticks he tied to the line would make a small noise that would give him time to act. It wasn't perfect, but it was better than nothing.

He took out his phone and powered it up.

Awaiting extraction

His phone vibrated immediately, and he answered it.

"Authenticate Hate."

"Power."

"Where the fuck are you?" Fury growled.

"We just made it to Tiksi. We're in one of the

Potemkin structures along the shore. Rostova's group has just left, heading toward Nayba."

"We'll get the boat there ASAP."

"There's no way a boat is going to make it to this port." Mal closed his eyes. He was exhausted.

"An icebreaker will. There's one attached to the Russian science outpost on Yalutia. It'll be coming in to do its paperwork, and the KGB officer has to swear all occupants of the island are still there prior to his departure. When the ship is being restocked, you will pick up something and carry it aboard."

"I believe it's FSB now, and you meant to say *we* will go onboard."

"The damn letters don't mean fuck-all. It's still the state police. One person is the agreed upon transit."

"Then you better get through to them and agree on two. She's coming with me." He wasn't going to leave her. "She saved my ass."

"In order to save her own, no doubt." Fury's voice was deadly cold. "This is risky enough with one. Two will be next to impossible, and she might not survive what you'll have to endure to get back."

"She's survived the Siberian winter during a

fucking hurricane running from people who would kill her. She'll manage."

"Impossible," Fury spat out again.

"Then find a way that is possible. She *is* coming with me." Mal hung up on the ancient assassin. Leaving her was not an option. And no, he didn't want to acknowledge the reason was partly his attraction, but it was. That made no fucking sense, but he had nothing to refute the fact that he was interested in her. Beyond interested, which bothered him. He hadn't had the bandwidth to think too much about it. Surviving the trek there had taken all his concentration. Then, there was the fact she'd saved his ass. Which, if his little head wasn't thinking for his big head, he'd admit was the primary reason she deserved a way out of that hell. He made sure his tripwires were intact and made his way back into the box and to the shelter. He shoved his pack in, crawled inside, checked the load on his weapon, turned the selector to auto, and dropped his head onto his arm as he stretched out. Sleep didn't take long to arrive.

"I REALLY NEED to remind these motherfuckers who and what I am," Fury said between clenched teeth. If one more son of a bitch hung up on him, he would explode.

"You promised Mom no more missions," Blake said from behind him. Somehow, the man-child had snuck up on him.

"Boy, do not make me take you out of this world." Fury turned to look at his son, who was just as tall and almost as broad as he was.

Blake gave a low laugh. The same scary as fuck laugh as his. "Right. You've taught me everything you know. Do you actually think you could?" Blake turned and sauntered out of the room.

Fury smiled, turning back to his desk. *Yeah, I could.* For now. In a couple of years, probably not. Blake was strong and smart, and he had the right mentality to continue in his father's footsteps. Ember would have a fit when the time came, but he and Blake had talked for hours about Blake's future, along with Fury's past, what he was, and what he'd done. He hadn't hidden a damn thing from the kid. They also discussed what Blake wanted to do with his life.

Fury picked up the phone and pushed a button.

When he took his last breath, Guardian would be in good hands.

"What's up, Joseph?" his brother asked in lieu of a greeting.

"Jacob, you need to get ahold of that contact of Tori's in the CIA. We need transport for two passengers out of Tiksi, and they need to work it ASAP. There's an active search underway for our asset."

CHAPTER 9

*A*nya woke slowly. The type of waking that steps out of a cloud. She opened her eyes and blinked. The digital camouflaged snow pattern of Mal's jacket was right in front of her eyes. She shifted a bit, and the rigor of the last couple of days made itself known. Her neck, back, and legs ached. She curled her toes in her felt boot liners. She needed to darn her socks. She could feel a blister that had formed from a hole in her left sock, but she'd made the trek.

"Good morning."

Anya turned over. "You gave me your jacket?" She pushed the material out of the way.

"I wasn't cold, and you were huddled up like a

closed fist." Mal handed her a canteen cup. "Coffee."

"Oh." Anya sat up and took the silver-colored tin cup. "Thank you." She took a sip and sighed. "It has been a long time. How long have you been awake?"

"Several hours," Malice said as he started to remove pouches from a big, heavy plastic bag. "Breakfast," he said as she watched him. "Unfortunately, this is beef stew, not eggs and bacon."

"What are you doing?" she asked as he poured a bit of water into a bag.

"Heating it up." He dropped a tablet into the water, and it started to boil. He put the smaller unopened bag in the pouch and crimped the top. "You don't have these?"

"No."

"What did you eat for rations in the field?"

"What we could carry." She took two pouches from him when he offered it. More times than not, they went without much food in the field when she was in the military. As a member of Rostova's group, food was available.

"Crackers. This is peanut butter. I'm sorry the fare isn't grander."

"This is good." Anya took another sip of her coffee. "Rostova's group?"

"I haven't heard any snow machines come back yet."

"Are there any in town?"

"Probably. I haven't ventured far. Especially not in this." He waved at his high-tech clothes.

Anya ate her crackers by squirting the thick peanut butter out of the smaller packet and smearing it across the top of the crispy layer. The food was dry but good. She took a long drink of her coffee. The steam was still visible from the liquid. "Is there a way to leave?" she asked as she brushed the cracker crumbs off her lap.

"Yes, my organization is working on the particulars now." Mal pulled the pouch out of the steamy water and opened it. He handed it to her and a plastic spoon. She dipped the spoon in and tried the gravy. It wasn't bad, but … "Not like babushka used to make."

Malice chuffed out a laugh. "No doubt, but it's full of calories and will keep you going."

"Are you going to eat?"

"After you're done." He frowned and patted his side. A phone she hadn't seen before was in his hand.

He put it up to his ear after swiping the face. "Go. Hate."

Anya lifted her eyebrows at the awkward word but kept eating the stew. She watched as Malice listened. "When?" He glanced at her, then back down to the shiny silver blanket they were sitting on. "How?"

He closed his eyes and sighed. "Thanks for that." A smile crept across his expression. "I understand." Malice took the phone away from his ear.

"We're leaving soon."

"How are we to do this?" She scraped the bottom of the pouch for the last of the food.

Malice looked at her. "I'm not at liberty to say until we need to move."

Anya licked her white plastic spoon. "You do not trust me."

"My leadership doesn't know you." He shrugged.

"Ah." She put the pouch with food down. "Do you?"

"Better than they do."

"What do you know about me?" she asked as he opened a thin box and took out more packets, going through the same process to warm his breakfast.

"You're a talented marksman. You're a fighter. You didn't let your spotter, who was three times your size, kill you. You're analytical. You debate what to say in your head before you let it out of your mouth. You aren't sure if I'm actually taking you with me, and if I do, you're not sure what will await, but you're willing to risk it to find a better path."

Anya studied him. He was intelligent and observant, but so was she. He was a distraction, too. She would be lying if she didn't admit she'd felt his body's reaction to sleeping together. If there hadn't been a motor, would she have moved against him? Probably. She hadn't been with a man in a very long time. And Mal was candy to a starving child. She wanted to taste him. But survival and escape tempered her desires as they should. So, she shrugged. "And will there be a better path?" She watched him drop a tablet into the pouch and place his food inside, sealing it up again.

"That depends on you." Mal took a drink from the canteen that held their water. "I was just told you're my responsibility."

Anya swallowed the coffee she was drinking. "Meaning what?" She was responsible for herself.

"That if you're a Russian agent, if you do anything that jeopardizes our safety, our extraction, or my organization, I am to take care of you." Malice squeezed his peanut butter onto his cracker. "You understand what that means, of course." His eyes lifted to hers. "Please don't make me do that. I think I could like you."

Anya drew a deep breath and stared at the American before her. "I want to leave Russia. I will not be a hindrance. I am not a threat to you or your agency. But if you come after me, I will fight back. And I could like you, too. For an American, you are not so bad." She lifted her chin in a bit of defiance.

Malice shoved the cracker into his mouth and chewed as he stared at her. He took a drink of water before he spoke. "I didn't think you would be a threat. But you asked me to not treat you like a simpleton, so I told you the truth. For a Russian, you're not so bad either."

"The truth is necessary." She nodded. "That is why I spoke mine."

Mal opened the pouch where his food had been warming. She watched as he consumed his food far faster than she had. A scrape alongside the building drew her attention. His hand was on her arm in an instant.

She looked at him, and he held up his finger over his mouth. Carefully, he grabbed her rifle and handed it to her before picking up his. He pushed back the flap of the shelter and exited soundlessly. Anya did the same. She wrapped her arm around her rifle's sling, using it as a support, and moved to the right as Mal moved to the left.

She heard the men talking. They were bitching about the cold, which was comical because, after the storm, the temperatures had been mild. The sound of someone pounding on plywood echoed through the fake structure. The wall beside her reverberated.

"There is no one. Why did he send us down here?"

"Because he wants to sit in the warm and fill his stomach with food and vodka. If we die and do not come back, more food for him," the other said. "Look, here. A way in."

"Maybe we stay inside and let him find us," the first man said.

"He would not look." The other laughed. One man pushed through the opening. Mal was behind him in an instant. His hand clamped over the man's mouth and chin. The other palmed the back of his head. If Anya had blinked, she would have missed the instantaneous snap of the man's neck. Mal controlled the man's fall to the ground.

"What do you see?" the second man asked as he pushed his way through. The American grabbed the man by the head, locking the Russian in a bend forward. Mal's hand covered the man's mouth, and a knife Anya had seen when Mal had sharpened it slit the man's throat. A rush of air was the only sound before Malice dragged the dead man from the passage to the outside.

Anya slid out of the small opening of the plywood box they were in and dropped to the ground. She let her eyes adjust before moving out. She listened and carefully moved around the building. Her leg encountered resistance as she edged forward, and she stopped. Carefully, she lowered and felt for whatever was pushing against her clothing. She felt the line and followed it to a clump of sticks that were placed beside the building. Ah, the American had set traps either that morning or last night.

She spun at a sound behind her. Mal lifted a hand and motioned for her to go right. She nodded and moved forward, careful to lift her leg over the line that attached to the sticks. She moved to the outskirts of the fake village, then moved back in. There was no one else. She stopped and stared at the little town. Electric lights cast a yellow haze from the buildings. A few dogs yapped, and a snow machine started but drove away from where she was concealed. The distant sound of laughter met her ears. No one in the town knew they were waiting or that two men had died.

She scanned the village. When her gaze reached the port, she blinked. *What ...*

A hulking shadow moved slowly from the darkness. The lights at the port turned on, illuminating a heavy hulled transport ship. Ice curled up and away from the bow. The sound of ice grinding against metal rumbled the ground beneath her feet. She backed deeper into the shadows as people spilled out of the buildings around the port. Men rushed to positions and shouted directions.

"Our ride."

Anya spun, grasping her chest. "Holy Mother of God, you cannot do that!" She jacked the words off in Russian. She gasped and dropped against the shell of a building that hid them both from view. "How do you move with no sound when you are so big?"

"Practice," the American said. "We need to be ready."

"For what?"

"They will start loading the ship. We will fall into the line and go aboard." Mal's eyes narrowed. "The Rostova Group will know you're missing by now and know that your rifle took out several of the men."

Anya didn't doubt it. She was a marked woman. Karl Rostova would no doubt pay well for her return. She'd die slowly if she were taken back.

"I've got an idea." Mal turned to her. "Let's get ready."

She narrowed her eyes at the silent and deadly man who walked in front of her. He'd been completely truthful with her, and if he wanted to, he could have killed her a hundred times over. She, too, could have killed him. Her revolver was deadly when she could aim it.

CHAPTER 10

*a*nya shook her head. "It will not work."

"It *will* work," Malice said as he helped her take off her old reindeer hide coat. It was cold and dark outside the plywood box, but they couldn't get out of the damn thing rigged up the way they needed to be. The warp in the wall was too narrow.

Anya repeated, "You will not fit."

"I'll make it work." He hoped. He gave her his jacket and insulated pants.

"Oh, this is warm," she purred as she slipped into the pants and coat.

He shivered as the cold ran through the layers of clothes he wore under the outer shell. "You look like a baby wrapped in blankets."

Anya snapped her head up. "I am not a baby. I am a woman." She raked her eyes up and down his frame. "And you are a man. A very big man. You will not fit in my clothes."

"They're enormous to make room for your layers. Watch." He pulled on her outer layer of reindeer hide pants. They barely made it to his hips, and if he took too long of a step, they'd split.

"The boots," Anya said. "Here. I can wrap them in this." She unwrapped her rifle. The white canvas material was in one long strip. She cut it in half and wound it around his brand-new, high-tech boots. "This will do," she said, looking up at him from her knees in front of him. Mal felt a zing of completely misplaced lust run through his body and shoved that bastard right back down into the crazy pit it came out of.

"Coat." She stood up and helped him put the coat on. It would work if he didn't bend down too far. The seams at the shoulders and back fought against him. She helped him put on her hat and fur scarf, winding the latter around the bottom of his face to complete the look.

"You will not be able to pick me up," Anya said. "The pants are too tight. You cannot move your arms."

"Stand up and grab the canvas tarp." Malice moved over to her. He lifted the tarp about two feet over her head. "Grab this corner." He handed it to her, then proceeded to spin her into the tarp. "All right, I'm going to bend as far down as I can. When I say jump, hop up onto my shoulder."

Anya mumbled something in Russian. "What did you say?"

"I feel like a pierogi," she said louder.

Malice couldn't help the smile that spread across his face. "Ready?"

"No," she sassed.

Malice bent as far as he could in the pants. "Jump."

He rammed his shoulder forward. The oomph of her losing her air did not escape him. He straightened and tossed her a bit higher, then settled her on his shoulder. She barely weighed anything. "Are you okay?"

He heard a liturgy of angry Russian cuss words. He made sure his hat was on and jiggled her again. "I do not like leaving my rifle," Anya complained.

"Nor do I, but it would be a bit obvious. At least we're able to keep your scope." It was in one of the pockets of the coat Anya currently wore. He walked around the building and toward the dock.

The arrival of the ship had put the small, sleepy village into overdrive. Mal timed his move to fall in behind the last of the men taking boxes onto the ship.

A man walking along the dock stopped when he passed. "You. Wait."

Mal kept walking. He looked up the ramp ahead of him. Fifty feet. They were less than fifty feet from safety. *Damn it.* The man grabbed his arm. "Are you deaf?" The man wore the emblem of the Rostova Group.

"No," Mal replied in Russian.

"Is there a problem?" a commanding voice from the gangplank asked.

Mal glanced over and did a double take. An FSB officer casually strolled down the ramp. The Rostova man pointed to Mal. "I do not recognize him."

The FSB officer looked up at Mal. "And this matters to me, how?"

"We are searching for people," the man blustered. "Colonel Rostova was murdered."

The FSB officer tipped his head to the side and stared at the Rostova man. "I heard, but I assure you the crew of this ship is not involved. Unless you think three new rugs for the outpost were used to kill your colonel."

Mal plastered a look of complete disinterest on his face, but the FSB officer vouching for him was more than a shock. The Rostova man swore bitterly before he turned and stomped away. "You. Follow me." The FSB officer turned on his heel and made his way up the gangplank.

Mal fell into step behind the man. The officer led him down into the cargo hold, past the men stacking the items from the warehouse. At the end of the bay, the FSB officer used a set of keys and unlocked another area. "In here."

Mal stooped through the door, and a few of the stitches in the back of Anya's coat popped. The FSB officer shut the door behind them. In English, he said, "My name is Renat. You'll be safe here. This is my private area reserved for my ... friends while we're in port. No one will disturb you. The bathroom is through there. I'll bring food as I can. We will continue on our mission, and you will not come out of here until I tell you. At the point where you can be evacuated from the ship, I will do so. You should probably put this one down."

Malice stared at the man, not saying a word. The FSB officer lifted an eyebrow and sighed. "Fine. Angels come from heaven." The man quoted the first part of the phrase he was supposed to hear when meeting his contact.

"As do Guardians," Malice finished. He bent over, and several more stitches of Anya's coat snapped free. He held Anya until she was stable, then helped unravel the worn canvas. She tripped and almost fell, but he held her arm as she freed herself from the drape of material. Her hair fell around her shoulders, and her cheeks were bright red, probably from being draped over his shoulder.

"My contact did not say a woman would be onboard." The FSB officer stared at Anya, and Malice did not like the type of look he leveled at her. Malice moved directly in front of the officer. The man shifted to look around Malice. Mal side-stepped, blocking his view again. The woman who had helped him escape an almost certain injury, if not death, did not deserve to be subjected to yet another leer from another man. Renat frowned and looked up at him. Malice met his glare with one of his own and asked, "Does it matter?"

"No. It does not," Renat said and smiled. "Just a nice deviation. You are important people, as the CIA has pulled in many favors to get you out of Russia. Did you kill Rostova?"

"If you were supposed to know, you would

have been briefed, just as I would have been." Malice was done playing with the man. "You've been paid."

"Very well." The man smiled. "This is the key for the door. Please lock it from the inside. I will knock twice. Do not answer unless it is twice. I'll bring food and clothing soon. The shower is that way. Please do not leave this area. The men will not come in here, but they will report seeing strangers on board. Then I will have to act."

Once the man had left, it took him a hot minute to get out of Anya's clothes. They were too tight and stuck. She helped him pull the clothing off, and it turned inside out as they tugged to get it off. He shed most of his outer clothes as the room was warm. He heard Anya taking off her clothes, too. He turned around and did a double take. She'd stripped down to what looked like a dark brown pair of long winter underwear. Her body under the form-fitting shirt and pants was long and lean. The swell of her chest caught his attention, but it was the cut from her collarbone down past the covering of the neckline of the undershirt that held his attention. He stood up and moved her hair off her shoulder where it was covering the wound. "Your spotter did this?"

She glanced down at the cut. "Yes. He came at me with a knife. The reindeer hide saved me."

"It's infected." He pulled the neck of her shirt down a bit. The red puffiness around the stitches was worrisome, as were the thin lines of red that spidered out from the wound.

Anya moved away from his touch. "I will shower. It will be fine."

"Let me make sure it's safe first." Mal headed toward where Renat had indicated. He stopped at the door and blinked. There was a commode, a sink, and a drain on the floor. A hose ran from the sink to the floor by the drain.

"Oh, wonderful," Anya said from behind him. "Do you think they have hot water?" She pushed past him and quickly ensured the hose was affixed to the faucet. "Soap," she said and held up a bar of it. "It is a good day."

Malice smiled and nodded. "You go first."

"Are you sure?" Anya twisted to look at him. "The water is hot."

"I'm sure." He shut the door behind him, giving her some privacy. The adequacy of the small bathroom was less than rudimentary, but she seemed happy with it. If that woman ever saw his bathroom at his house in Virginia, she'd have an aneurysm. His shower was twice the size of the bathroom she was currently luxuriating in. He had at least fifteen shower heads and two tankless hot water heaters that filled that shower with enough warmth to last for days.

Mal paced in the metal room as she showered. He hated being enclosed. Hated relying on someone he did not know. Granted, Guardian had vouched for the man, and the FSB officer had saved his bacon, but it was an uncomfortable situation.

Two knocks echoed from the door. Mal moved over and unlocked it. He stood behind the door as it opened, Anya's revolver in his hand. Renat shut the door behind him. He glanced at the revolver and then at Malice. "I told you I would be back." He moved over to the table and set a large wooden box down on top of it. "In here is clothing and food. We will travel for four days before I will be back. I cannot change my habits, or the crew will know something is wrong. On the fourth day, you will wear the suits on the bottom of the box. You will put them on when you hear the horn blow three times. Then you will come out, go up the steps we came down, and turn right. Work your way to the back of the boat. I will meet you there. You will be put out on a covered life raft. Your people will pick you up, or you will freeze, but my job will be done."

"I understand."

"Lock the door after me. I will not come back. Do not answer if anyone knocks." Renat walked back to the door. "I can do nothing else for you."

The man left, and Malice locked the door behind him. Then he went back to the table and unloaded the box. A bottle of vodka lay on top of the clothes. Warm and clean, there appeared to be two sets of everything, and they both looked big enough for him to wear. Anya would swim in them, but she'd be warm. There were several bags of dried meat, a wheel of cheese with a knife, four loaves of bread, a spread of some sort in what looked like a canning jar, and a deck of cards.

Underneath that were two neoprene survival suits still in the bag the manufacturer had placed them in. The immersion suits would keep them alive if they plunged into the arctic waters. He moved those to the corner of the counter set up along one wall of the room before he took a change of clothes to Anya. He knocked on the door. It opened about two inches, and a very wet

Anya peeked out. "Clothes. I'll put them on the floor."

She nodded and shut the door quickly. He chuckled, then went back to the small counter area where he'd put the survival suits. He removed the supplies they'd shoved into his coat. Enough protein bars to sink a ship. He'd rather eat real food, but then again, he couldn't cook for shit, so he usually ate takeout. Her rifle's scope was placed next to the immersion suits.

By the time she walked out of the bathroom, he'd unpacked and organized everything. She'd cuffed the pants at the top and the bottom. The shirt's sleeves she'd pushed up into a wrinkled mess by her elbows. She was running her fingers through her hair. "I don't have a brush." She shrugged. It didn't matter. She was stunningly attractive. Her hair fell to her shoulders in curls, and the feminine form under the clothes couldn't be mistaken. Malice turned away. What had she said ... Oh, right. "Sorry, neither do I." Mal pointed at the counter. "Vodka, food, immersion suits." He pointed to each and then explained what Renat had told him about hearing the horn blow three times.

She nodded. "Shower, and I will make food for

us," Anya said. "The warm water is good for the body."

"Thanks. Don't open the door. Renat said he would not be back down." Malice grabbed the clean clothes and headed to the bathroom. The warm water was good, and the fact that there wasn't any showerhead on the end of the hose was interesting, but warm water and soap were a fucking beautiful thing when you hadn't showered in over a week. He glanced at himself in the small reflective piece of metal that was probably supposed to be a mirror. His beard had fully grown in, which he didn't mind. A woman he'd had relations with had once told him never to wear a beard because it made him look sinister. He smiled at his reflection. If she'd only known.

CHAPTER 11

*A*nya opened the vodka and found a paper napkin among the things stacked on the shelf above the counter. She carefully poured some of the alcohol on the napkin and slipped off her shirt. The stitches were infected. There was a yellowish pus toward the bottom of the cut that she'd washed off with soap. With care, she cleaned around the stitches and the wound with the vodka. It stung like a bitch, but it didn't matter. She needed to fight the infection and be strong. When she got to America, she'd ask for medication.

Anya tossed the napkin in the waste basket and put her shirt back on, turning her attention to the food Mal had put out on the counter. She cut off two slices of bread and covered each piece with a smear of the spread. She sliced the cheese and placed some meat on the spread before pouring some of the vodka. When Mal came out of the bathroom, she took a big sip from the cup. The material of the borrowed clothes fit tight against his strong body. His thighs were thick with muscle, as were his arms and chest.

Anya turned and pointed to the table. "Food and vodka." She offered him the cup.

"I'll take the food, but one of us should stay sober."

Anya pulled a face. "One glass of vodka does not make a person drunk." She laughed at him. She could drink Dima under the table and make sure they got home safely. She frowned at the thought. Dima had been a big part of her life, and she'd killed him. It was her or him, and she chose herself just as Dima had chosen his path.

"What happened just now?" he asked. "You went from happy to sad like that." He snapped his fingers.

"A memory of how choices change our lives." She shrugged and lifted the small glass. "To better times."

He nodded, and she tipped the glass back before she pointed to the table. "Food."

"What is this spread?" Mal asked. He sniffed the bread and took a tentative bite.

"Fat, herbs, some have vegetables." Her babushka had made a similar spread, too. It replaced butter in most homes in Siberia.

He took a bite, and his eyebrows rose. "Not bad."

Anya snorted. "You don't have this?" She sat down and took a slice of cheese for herself.

"We might?" Mal shrugged. "I don't cook much. If it can't be microwaved, I don't make it. I usually get takeout."

Anya stared at him. "You do not cook."

He shook his head. "Never learned, and I don't plan on learning."

"Cooking is about family. It is about traditions." Anya lifted her hands in the air. The pull on her stitches made her drop them into her lap. "Your mother did not have family recipes?"

Mal shook his head. "I never knew my mother or father. I grew up in a series of foster homes. I don't have any family traditions."

Anya blinked and stopped chewing as she digested that. "An orphan?"

"Something like that." Mal nodded and took another bite of his food. He didn't seem bothered by the topic, although Anya was sure for a moment that she'd stepped in the middle of a horrible mess.

She played with the cheese in her hand. "My babushka taught me how to cook. I miss it. I miss her."

"How long has she been gone?" Mal asked before he took another bite.

"Oh …" Anya stopped. "Has Christmas come this year?"

Mal nodded. "Five days ago."

"Then four years. She died on Christmas Day four years ago."

Mal stopped eating. "I'm sorry for your loss."

"She was over one hundred years old. She went to sleep and did not wake up. It was her time." Anya stared at her meat and bread. "She was a good woman."

"Like her granddaughter," Mal said.

"I kill people." Anya looked up at him. "This does not make me good."

"I disagree. You are very good at what you do. Did you make a mistake and align yourself with an organization that you shouldn't have? Yes. But you did what you did to survive. Good people make bad decisions all the time."

Anya took a sip of her vodka. "This is a different way to think about things."

"It's how I exist. I did a bad thing for a good reason, and I was caught. Now, I do the right thing for the right people, and I make sure little ones are safer."

"It is about the children for you." Anya nodded. He'd mentioned the children before. "You care for them."

"They don't have anyone to defend them." Mal shrugged. "If I can be that person, all the better."

"You have a woman, girlfriend, children?" Anya took another sip of the vodka.

"No. My profession isn't conducive to relationships."

Anya snorted and picked up a piece of cheese. Malice frowned at her. "What was that noise about?"

"Excuses," Anya said and popped the cheese into her mouth. She chewed it, then spoke again. "If you want this ... a relationship, you find a way to make it work."

Malice finished the bite that he was chewing. "You know this from experience?"

Anya stared at him. "No. But I have watched

those who care for each other. When the person is important, allowances are made."

Malice took the last bite of his meat and bread. When he finished, he stood up. "You may be right. Some people I know have juggled the profession and the relationship."

Anya nodded. "You just have not found the one you are willing to make an allowance for. Neither have I. My babushka said when you know, you know." She took a bite of her bread and meat and pushed the cheese tray over to his side of the table. He came back with a glass of water for himself and the vodka bottle. "Another?"

"Little bit." She pushed her glass over to him. "Where do you live in America?"

"I have several homes. Most of the time, I'm in Virginia." Malice took a slice of the cheese.

"Where is this?" She took another bite of her food.

"On the East Coast of the nation. Near Washington, DC," Malice answered.

"Where will they make me live?"

"Make you? No one is going to make you live anywhere. I expect as soon as you're cleared by Guardian, you could live wherever you want."

And that caught her attention. She jerked, straightening in her chair. She hissed a bit and curved forward to relieve the tension on her stitches. "Cleared by Guardian. I'm going to go to prison?"

Malice frowned. "No. Why would you go to prison? Are you okay?"

"Fine. You said cleared. To be cleared, you must go to prison, yes? Have I got it right?"

Malice shook his head. "No, you do not. Guardian will make sure you aren't a threat. They'll sponsor you into the country, so you're there legally. I expect they'll help you get a job and settle."

"Ah, blat," Anya said. That made sense. She'd owe this Guardian.

"No." Malice laughed. "Nothing like that. The company has integrity. If they're going to bring you into the country, they're going to make sure you're a good fit."

"And if I don't fit?" Anya leaned forward. She pushed what was left of her food away from her.

"They'll help you find a place where you're comfortable." Malice pointed to her bread and meat. "Are you going to eat that?"

She shook her head. Malice pulled the plate

toward him. "You winced earlier. May I look at your wound?"

Anya sighed and made a spinning motion with her finger, asking him to turn around. Malice picked up her plate, stood, and spun around. She heard him take a bite as she pulled off the shirt and then wrapped it around her chest, so her breasts weren't exposed. "All right."

Malice turned around and blinked. "Fuck me."

Anya flinched at the remark but tried to make light of it. "That is not an entirely objectionable thought, but I don't think that is what you meant." Anya looked down at her stitches. The red was brighter, and the pus was forming again.

"*Shit*. No, it wasn't. Hold on." Malice tossed the plate to the table. It landed with a loud clatter as he jogged over to his coat. He lifted several of the tabs on the numerous pockets of his jacket until he pulled out a red zipper pouch.

The engines of the boat increased in vibration and noise. "We're leaving," Malice said before turning and pointing to the bed. "Come over here to the bed and lie down."

Anya cocked her head. "Lie down? Or *was* it what you meant?"

Malice blinked, then laughed. "I have antibiotics, antibiotic ointment, and bandages. Let me play doctor."

Anya couldn't hide the smile. "Play doctor? In Russia, I think this means something different from America, yes?"

Mal sighed and shook his head, but the laugh was still there. "Stop making this awkward."

Anya walked over and looked up at him as she passed. "It *is* awkward. I'm not making it so."

"True." Malice opened the pouch and unfolded it. "Okay. Let's get this taken care of." He put on a pair of blue gloves and started opening little packets. "The streaks going away from the wound worry me." He used an alcohol pad and wiped around the stitches.

"Dima's knife was dirty. Rusty. He did not care for his weapons."

"And your hands were probably dirty when you were sewing yourself back together." Malice replaced the pad with a cotton swab and cleaned around the thread.

"There wasn't time to find a wash basin." Anya's response was curt. She'd done the best she could in the situation.

Malice looked up from his work. "I wasn't criticizing you. Anyone who can stitch themselves together in the middle of the Siberian winter is a baller in my book."

Anya frowned at him. "What does that mean?"

"A baller?"

She nodded.

Malice smiled. She was close enough to notice the dark ring around his hazel-colored eyes. "Baller means something excellent or a successful person."

"Ah. It means athlete in Russia."

"I'm going to go deep here to see if I can clean out some of this infected area." Malice put his glove-clad fingers on the top of her breast to move it away so he could see. "Sorry."

"Do what you need to do." She wasn't shy but preferred to be appropriate. Her life since being in the military had left little room for modesty. She hissed and tightened her body as he cleaned the area.

"So, not too objectionable, huh?" Malice said as he concentrated on what he was doing.

What? Oh. Anya opened her mouth to speak and then snapped it shut when he worked on her wound. She mentally swore a thousand curses as he worked. Tears streamed from the corners of her eyes.

"Done. I'll put some ointment on it now."

She waited for him to look at her, not her wound. When he did, she lifted an eyebrow and said, "I could think of worse things to do."

Malice threw her a questioning look, but her answer dawned on him. He tossed back his head and laughed. "You're amazing for my ego."

"Ego? A man like you should have no problem with your ego. You have the stable, right?" The ointment was cool as he spread it along the wound.

"Stable? You mean many women?" He opened a packet and took out two pieces of gauze.

"Yes. At your command." She was sure he only had to lift a finger, and a woman would drop to her back and spread her legs.

"No. Absolutely not." Malice chuckled as he measured medical tape the length of the pads.

"Really?" she said disbelievingly.

"I'm not a saint, but I'm not a manwhore either." Malice worked as he talked. "I want to mark the red streaks." He got up, went to the shelves, and brought a ballpoint pen back. He drew a line near the top of the longest of the red lines before putting the bandage over her wound. "I have antibiotics, too." Malice put his medical bag back together and turned around. "You can get dressed now."

Anya sat up and put the shirt back on. "It is safe," she said as she was pushing the extraordinarily long sleeves up her arm.

"I think you should take these until we can get you real medical help." Malice shook out two of the tablets. "Although you probably shouldn't take them with alcohol."

Anya took the tablets and walked to the table, downing the tablets with what was left of her vodka. "Americans worry too much."

Malice chuckled from behind her. "Not really." He put the kit on the counter. "Have you ever played poker?"

Anya turned with her empty cup still in her hand. "Poke her?" She blinked at him innocently.

Malice dropped his head and groaned. "I think you have sex on the brain."

Anya deadpanned, "No, I have sex on the bed. The table, the floor … not the brain."

"And with that, I'll teach you how to play five-card draw."

Anya sat down at the table. "I prefer stud."

Malice's jaw dropped open. His face turned red under that bushy beard of his. Anya laughed.

She was embarrassing the assassin. "You are blushing."

Malice shook his head. "Normally, I'm the one handing out the corny lines."

"Corny?" She looked across the table at him.

"Ah … never mind. I don't have a definition for that."

Anya took the deck of cards from him and shuffled them. "What are we playing for?"

Malice stared at her for a moment before he suggested, "Bragging rights?"

Anya shook her head. "There has to be something on the line to make it worth our while."

"Okay, how about this? When we get back to the States, the person who loses the most games has to cook the person who wins the most games dinner."

"But you do not cook," Anya said and lifted her eyebrows.

Malice leaned back in his chair and gave her a smug smile. "And I don't intend on losing either."

She narrowed her eyes at him, then lifted a finger and pointed directly at him. "I will cook for you if I lose. If I *win*, you will take me to a fancy American restaurant. I want the best."

Malice extended his hand. "Deal."

Anya reached over and grabbed his hand. A zap of pure excitement screamed up her arm when she shook his hand. As she started to deal, she thought that maybe sex with him would be a good time. A very good time.

CHAPTER 12

Malice held two pairs, aces, and fives. They'd found some match sticks to bet with, although they were only keeping track of the number of games won, not the pile of sticks that moved between them. When she was low, he gave her a handful. When his pile ran low, she returned the favor. He yawned and glanced at the clock that hung on the wall. "Last hand and then sleep?"

Anya nodded. "You take the bed. I will sleep on the floor."

"Like hell, you will." Malice didn't put any steam in the statement, but he'd be damned if that would happen.

Anya tossed five sticks into the pile. "What does that mean?"

"The bed is big enough for us to sleep together." Malice didn't relish the idea of sleeping on the metal floor either.

Anya turned around and looked at the bunk, then spun back to face him. "Are we talking about the same bed?"

He chuckled, called, and put his hand down. "Two pairs. Aces and fives."

Anya sighed. "That is a good hand." She paused. "Mine is better." She put down a full house.

Malice groaned and added another tick to her win column. "Are you cheating?"

She snorted. "I do not need to cheat. I will be back." She made her way to the bathroom, and Malice went to the medical kit to get two more tablets for her. He had enough for one more day. Hopefully, whatever was in the pills would kick her wound's infection or slow it down. He'd seen worse infections, but not by much. Keeping it clean would help, but damn it, this was bad.

Anya came back into the room. "How are we both going to sleep on this bed?" She looked from the bed to him.

"Easy." He walked past her, pulled the blanket

down, and got in. He pushed against the wall and patted the mattress beside him. "You sleep here."

"There was more room in the emergency shelter." Anya shook her head but headed to the light switch. She turned it off, and Malice waited for his eyes to adjust to the darkness. He felt her run into the bed and heard her swear in Russian. He held out his hand and found her. She grabbed his hand and slipped into bed with him.

After covering them with the harsh wool blanket, Malice settled down on the pillow they now shared. "Thank you for taking care of my wound."

"You should have let me know it was festering sooner." He adjusted a bit on his hip and drew a deep breath. "We're together in this."

She hummed something soft. He didn't question her. Exhausted from a hard mission and little sleep, Malice gratefully closed his eyes and went to sleep to the rhythmic sound of the boat's engines turning.

MALICE'S EYES POPPED OPEN. The darkness of the room and the sound of the boat engines hadn't changed, but something had. He held still while his brain sorted out why he woke. Then he knew. Anya's body was too warm. The ship was almost warm but not comfortable. The thick clothes and wool socks he wore shielded him from the chill, but beside him, she had turned into a furnace. He could see her in the faint light that came from under the door. He placed his hand on her forehead. A fever. It wasn't extreme, but she was warm. He dropped his head back on the pillow, and she shifted, moving closer to him. He dropped his arm over her and closed his eyes. Four days until they were put off the boat. He'd use everything in his medical kit to keep her healthy. She had saved his ass, and on top of that, she was funny, irreverent, and just this side of too pretty. Her body was tight and lean, her intelligence was sharp, and she was fucking strong. He admired her, didn't he? Malice thought about that for a minute. Yeah, he did. Respected her, too. He could see Anya with his friends. He could see her giving as good as she got, and he knew Val would do the big sister thing. She was such a girly girl. Malice chuckled but then sobered. He honestly wished Anya could go shopping and buy whatever she wanted. He wished she could have nice things and be safe. His arm tightened a bit around her at the thoughts. He would love to take her to all the Florida amusement parks and protect her from the harsh realities she'd lived through.

He could hear Ice's voice in his mind. *Mother Mal.* He did feel like protecting her, true, but there were other feelings that had nothing to do with mothering. Anya ticked boxes for him, and hell yeah, he'd take her to bed and do more than sleep if things were different. They'd joked about sex all night, but damn it, sex with her could be amazing if she weren't sporting a five-inch-long wound that was infected and causing her to have a mild fever.

"You should be asleep," Anya said from somewhere near his chest.

"So should you," Mal replied.

"I have a fever."

"I know. I can get you something for it."

"No, it is just my body fighting the infection." Anya yawned and turned over, so he was spooning her. "Just keep me warm."

Malice wrapped himself around her back and pulled her into him. "Go to sleep. I've got you."

"Hmmm …" Anya yawned. "Nice." She pushed back a bit more and lifted the wool blanket to her shoulder. Malice tugged it up a bit more, and she snuggled down under the cover. Mal held her as she drifted back to sleep. She fit well against him. He closed his eyes and agreed with his Russian sniper. This was nice.

MAL LOOKED across the room at where Anya was sleeping. Today was the day they'd be slipped off the ship, and Anya's infection and fever had incrementally worsened. The antibiotics seemed to work while she was taking them, but that morning, she'd started to have muscle contractions, and her fever didn't lower with the over-the-counter pain relievers he had in his medical pouch. He'd kept the wound clean, but the infection was spreading. She said her chest and neck were numb at times and tingled at others. He ran his hands through his hair just as the horn of the boat sounded three times. Anya sat up, her eyes wild and her face flushed red from fever. "It is time."

"It is." He took her suit over to her and helped her into it. There were no smart comments about feeling like a pierogi this time. He left her sitting on the bed and scrambled into his suit, cramming what remained of the medical kit, his comm device, her scope, and his cell phone into his suit, using the medical pouch to hold it all.

He grabbed her by the hand. "Can you make it?"

"I will." She stood and headed to the door. Mal opened the door, dropped the key, and wrapped his arm around her waist. The pace he set was nonnegotiable. He half carried her up the stairs and out of the hold. He followed the directions and found Renat at the back of the boat.

"Down the stairs. The emergency raft is tied to the bay door. Release yourself when you are in. Do not activate the emergency beacon until we are out of the area. Two hours minimum." Renat handed him a package, which he took under the arm that wasn't supporting Anya. "Give this to your contact and tell your masters we are even."

Malice nodded, and they made their way down the interior stairs to the lowest level of the boat. He pulled the covered rubber raft closer, gave the package to Anya, and let her fall into the interior of the raft. Malice grabbed the rope, untied it, pulled the raft as close as he could get it, and jumped onto their survival raft.

Malice hurried to zip up the cover of the raft. The emergency beacon was attached to the bars, stretching the covering. Anya handed him the package. Her hands shook violently as she waited for him to take the small bundle. She huddled into a curled ball beside him.

Mal cussed under his breath. "Just a minute, Anya, I'll get you warmer."

Malice opened the package. It was an external drive. He checked it for any signs of tampering, but there were none evident. It wouldn't be past the realm of impossibility that Renat had given him a bomb. He shoved the device into his fucking orange gumby suit. The boat's engines started turning, and the raft tossed on the waves from the propulsion.

Malice took the medical kit out of his suit. He opened both of the emergency blankets and wound Anya up in them. He pulled her onto his lap and wrapped his arms around her. "Hang on, little one."

Anya nodded. "Just a walk across the ice," she whispered.

"That's it. Just a short walk."

He held her tightly until she started shaking.

"Anya, what's happening?"

She said something in Russian, then looked up at him. "Do not leave me. Please, stay with me."

"I'm not going to leave you." He held her

tighter. "I'm not going to leave." Her eyes rolled back, and she seized. Anya's entire body spasmed, locking and contracting. Fuck it. He wasn't going to wait any longer. He powered his cell phone up and called in.

"Operator Two Seven Four. Where do you need to be directed, Sunset Operative Nineteen?"

"I need Fury or Anubis, stat."

"Transferring now," the operator said without emotion. He closed his eyes and waited for what seemed like forever but was only a minute or so.

"Where are you?" Fury demanded.

"In the middle of the damn ocean. Anya is seizing. I need fucking help. I have some meds in the pack, but I don't know what they do. The contact said to not activate the beacon for two hours. I don't know if she has two hours. You have to get us off this raft and to a hospital immediately."

"Standby," Fury said.

"CCS," the woman's voice said a few seconds later.

"I need latitude and longitude on Sunset Operative Nineteen's satellite phone. Also, hook me up to the closest Mercy team to Alaska."

"Working it." The woman's voice was clipped, and he could hear a keyboard's rapid staccato clicking in the background. "Mercy team number sent. Do you need me to link them in?"

"Affirmative," Fury acknowledged.

"I have the location locked."

"Get a Coast Guard rescue helicopter heading their way."

"It's in international waters," the woman said.

"I don't give a fuck if it's the South China Sea, Button. Just get it done."

"We copy. Watch the tone, my brother." That was a man's voice. Malice had heard him before when the woman was online. Maybe he was one of her assistants.

"Mercy Team Five online," the CCS woman said.

Another woman's voice announced her presence, "This is Dr. Montrose."

"Mal, tell her what's going on."

"Doc, I have a female, twenty-seven years old. A five-inch slice from the collarbone to the top of her breast. The cut is infected and pus filled. She sewed herself up. She has had a low fever for the last four days, but it spiked yesterday, and over-the-counter pain relievers are not reducing it. I've given her all the stabilized antibiotics that were in my emergency medical pouch. Her chest is numb at times and, at times, tingly. There are red streaks coming from the wound. I was able to keep them from growing for a couple of days, but over the last two days, the streaks have extended. She just had a seizure, and her entire body was locked up. She's unconscious now."

"Get her to a hospital immediately."

"I'm in the middle of the fucking ocean!" Mal roared the words. He couldn't do a damn thing, and he was fucking sick about it.

"Coast Guard is en route," the CCS woman said.

"Okay, settle down. What caused the wound?" The doctor remained calm, which did absolutely fuck-all for his raging inability to help Anya.

"A knife. Someone was trying to kill her," Malice ground out.

"Okay. Do you know if she's had a tetanus shot?"

Mal sighed. "I have no clue."

"My initial suspicion is she's contracted tetanus. The cumulation of the symptoms seems to support that conclusion, but it could be several other things."

"You mean lockjaw? Fuck, she said the knife was dirty and rusty."

"Lockjaw would be one of the last symptoms, yes. The good news is it can be treated if we get to her in time, but any damage done to the nerves from the seizures could take substantial rehab," Dr. Montrose told him before asking, "CCS, can you tell me where the Coast Guard will be taking them?"

"I can get that information. One moment," the woman replied.

"Okay. I'll call ahead to the hospital and let them know what they have coming in. There is nothing you can do now except keep her as comfortable as possible," the doctor said. "If it's tetanus, we're in a race against time. If it's blood poisoning, we're pushing back against the same clock."

"CCS, inform the Coast Guard time is of the essence."

"We copy," the man in CCS replied.

"They'll be transporting to Norton Sound Regional Hospital in Nome," the woman said. "I'll send you the telephone number to the administrator's office and the Emergency Department."

Malice shifted his hold on Anya. Her eyes fluttered open, then closed. "We have a plan," Fury interrupted. "Execute it. Mal, stay on the line."

"CCS clear."

"Mercy Team Five clear."

"I'm here," Mal said.

"Did you receive—"

"An external hard drive, yeah. I got it." He knew Fury had to ask, but it was the last thing on his mind.

"Good. Keep it safe until I can get someone up to Alaska to recover it from you. I'm assuming you want to stay until …"

"She recovers? Yes, I won't leave her." *I promised her, and I keep my promises.*

There was silence for a moment. "She might not recover, my man. Tetanus is deadly."

Malice closed his eyes. "I know, but she will. She's strong. She saved my ass, and she's got spirit, Fury. She's …" *Perfect for me. Someone I want to get to know intimately. Important, and I don't understand how that happened so quickly.* None of those statements made it out of his mouth. "… She's strong."

"While you're with her at the hospital, I'll expedite her clearance, visa, or whatever we're doing to keep her in the country. I need to know if you think she's a threat."

"No, sir, I don't. She has no one left in Russia. She was used for her talent."

"Which is?" Fury asked.

"She's a sniper. I told you that when I called for extraction. She's a damn good one."

"And you don't think she's a plant to get into the States and perform a mission once here?"

Malice closed his eyes. "Fury, you have a devious fucking mind."

"I'm paid to think of things like this."

"Lucky you." Malice sighed. "No, I don't think she has an alternate reason for leaving Russia other than getting away from Karl Rostova, and I'll stand by that."

"How far will you go to prove it?"

"I'll sponsor her. I'll be the one responsible for taking her out if she goes rogue." He held her tight and shook his head. "She's not a plant."

"I'll work the sponsorship up the line. It will make her assimilation more palatable since we have so little of her background. The helicopter should be to you soon. Call me when you get to Nome."

"Understood."

"Mal?"

"Yes, sir?"

Fury spoke softly, "Sometimes people aren't as good as we want them to be."

Mal looked down at the woman in his arms. "And sometimes they're better than you've ever had the courage to hope for."

"And that is a solid truth. Whatever it takes, my man."

"As long as it takes." Mal disconnected and dropped his head back against the raft's cover. He looked up and asked the universe, "Please don't take too long."

CHAPTER 13

*M*al watched as the stretcher holding Anya lifted from the raft.

"I need to get you into a harness, sir," the rescue swimmer said, pulling his attention from the stretcher making its way up to the orange and white helicopter.

Malice took the harness from the man and snapped it into place. The rescue swimmer checked his hook-up situation, and when the wire was dropped again, both men hooked onto the wire and were lifted from the small raft.

Mal used the rail of the aircraft to step up and into the cabin. The rescue swimmer was in seconds after him, and both harnesses were shed. As soon as the door shut, the nose of the helicopter dipped, and they were racing over the water.

Mal watched as the medic worked. He'd already peeled Anya out of the Gumby suit and, he assumed, had taken her vitals. He was handed a helmet, and once it was on, the medic talked to him. "I was told this could be a tetanus or blood poisoning situation. My station doc instructed an IV with a sedative that will help slow or control the muscle spasms she's experiencing. The ICU at Nome is aware and is on the horn in case she seizes again. How long was the last seizure?"

"At least a full minute," Mal replied. The longest fucking minute of his life. He answered several more questions and managed to grab Anya's hand when the medic moved a bit.

"What's her name?" the medic asked as he typed on a small computer.

"Anya Baranov."

"Age is twenty-seven, correct?"

"Correct."

"Address?"

Mal blinked up at the man. "Sorry?"

"Her address in the States? This is not only for our reports, but we'll forward it to the hospital, too."

Mal gave him his address in Virginia. He didn't have the bandwidth to give the man a fake address. He then answered the same questions about himself. It was interesting that not once was he asked how they got into the middle of the ocean or on a Russian life raft.

The helicopter veered. Mal looked out of the window and saw land. "Thank God."

"Nah, thank our pilot, Lieutenant Colonel Sanderson. She's the best helicopter pilot in the service." That came from the rescue swimmer.

Mal nodded. "Then my thanks go out to Colonel Sanderson, too."

A woman's voice came over the comms. "You're welcome. You're lucky you weren't out on that raft a week ago. We had one hell of a hurricane blow through."

Mal looked down at Anya. Was it only last week? The days had blurred together. The last two had been agonizingly long. He never wanted to feel that helpless again. He did what he could to help her, but it wasn't enough. When she seized in his arms, he'd been terrified. It had been one hell of a long time since he felt the kind of fear that had gripped his gut. And it still hadn't loosened its hold. Anya had wormed her way past the armor he used to keep people at a distance. Sure, according to Ice, he mothered people, and he'd own that particular trait. He cared for people who had no one else to do so.

Anya fit into that description, but his feelings for her were different. What had started as a truce between unknowns had morphed into respect. From there, it had grown into a friendship of sorts. Not the longtime friendships he had with his class but more of a natural feeling that the universe had put her in front of him for a reason. He enjoyed her company and sense of humor. He was interested in more, but that was a conversation he needed to have with her when she was healthy.

The helicopter landed a few minutes later, and Malice was out of the chopper and following the medical team that had been waiting for them. The medic from the Search and Rescue team moved with the medical personnel.

He was stopped at a set of double swinging doors. "Sir, could you come with me? I'll get her insurance information from you."

Malice blinked down at that woman. "What?"

"She's going to go through an evaluation, and the doctors are going to be with her for some time.

Come with me, and I'll get her insurance informa-tion and maybe some scrubs for you?"

He looked down at his immersion suit and the Russian clothes underneath. "I want to know what's happening in there." He pointed to the door.

The woman looked over her shoulder at the door. "Sir, my administrators told the entire emer-gency department that you were to be given immediate updates. You'll know what's going on, I promise. But until then, let's get the paperwork done and give the doctors time to take care of your wife."

Malice blinked down at her. "What?" Why would anyone say Anya was his wife? Ah, only family could be apprised of her medical situation. That had to be it.

"The doctor who called said you could provide the information."

"Right. Okay." Mal nodded. "What do you need?"

The nurse led him down the hall to the nurses' station. Mal filled out the forms, listing Anya's full name but using all the information he'd use if he needed to go to the hospital on downtime, as Guardian had trained them to do. The insurance company was a front as far as he was aware. He'd never questioned the mechanics behind Guardian's payment of bills. Then again, he'd never used the local hospitals. Guardian docs gave him his physicals and any inoculations he needed when he traveled. The nurse gave him a pair of scrubs and showed him to a room where he could change. He shoved the hard drive in the shirt's chest pocket, his comm box and cell phone in his pants pockets, and was back at the double doors within ten minutes. A doctor came out soon after that. "Mr. Baronov? I'm Dr. Lucas Pine."

"Baronov is her last name, not mine," Mal said. He extended his hand. "Mel Adams." All his real-world paperwork was in that name. It wasn't his real name, but no one would ever be able to determine that fact. Mel Adams didn't exist except to own property and hold investments.

The doctor shook his hand. "But you're her husband, correct?"

"Yes." According to the Guardian doctor, so that was what he was going with.

"Your wife has tetanus. We've started her with a course of antibiotics and, of course, given her a tetanus shot. Do you know when the last time she was inoculated?"

"I don't know that she ever was. She grew up in

Russia, and we were there until recently." Which wasn't a lie.

"All right. We're moving her up to the ICU. She's in critical condition, but we think we have a good plan going forward. How did she get the cut?"

"Someone attacked her. The cold-weather gear she was wearing saved her." Again, the truth.

"Have you filed a police report?"

"It happened in Russia. A police report wouldn't do any good."

The doctor frowned and stared at the floor. "And the stitches?"

"She sewed her wound together."

The doctor narrowed his eyes at Mal. "And where were you?"

"Dr. Pine, a moment?" A man wearing a gray suit and another gentleman wearing a black suit strode up to the doctor.

"In a minute, I need to get some answers." The doctor turned back to Mal. "Where were you?"

Mal narrowed his eyes and gave the doctor a look that made most men tremble. "I'm not inclined to say."

"Dr. Pine! Now," the admin type commanded. The doctor spun and walked away from him with the other two men. Mal crossed his arms and watched the conversation. Dr. Pine stepped back from the other two men and looked over at him. Mal cocked his head. What had he been told to give him a thunderstruck expression? The doctor wiped his face and nodded. He turned and walked back into the hall he'd exited from.

Mr. Black Suit came over. "Sir, I'm Nolan Sailor, the Supervisory Agent here at the FBI's Nome detachment. I'm sorry I didn't get here sooner. You nor your wife will have any more questions about the situation that brought you here. I have agents who will post out in front of the ICU or the ward until your wife is discharged, as requested. If you need anything from me, you can call me at this number." He handed Mal his card. "That's my direct number. No switchboards or answering services. Also, your headquarters wanted you to know Oscar Team was going to be here within the next three hours. They asked that you call once you felt safe leaving your wife."

"Thank you." Mal took the card from the man. "I'll call in shortly."

"If you need anything, don't hesitate. I've worked with your organization. I owe a Guardian my life."

Mal lifted an eyebrow in question. Nolan shook his head. "A long story and you have other things to tend to. I can take you up to the ICU. Unfortunately, I know where that's at."

"Part of that owing a Guardian your life comment?" Mal asked as he strode alongside the agent.

"It was." Nolan led him through the maze until they reached another set of metal double doors. "When everything's settled, her name will show here." He pointed to the screen above the television in the waiting room. "When you see it, you can go to the door, and they'll let you in. Normally, they won't let you stay with her, but I've talked to the administration. As long as you let the doctors and nurses do what they need to do, you can stay. They might ask you to leave for a short time, but you can come back in when they're finished."

"Thank you." Mal extended his hand. "Damn glad that Guardian saved your ass."

Nolan laughed. "So am I. Call if you need me. My agent will be here shortly."

Mal nodded and watched the man walk away. He dropped into a chair and stared at the monitor above the television. His eyes drifted down, and the news channel on the screen caught his attention.

He stood up and moved to the television, pushing the button at the bottom of the screen to turn it up. "Reports are conflicting at this time. However, it appears that the Rostova Group, a paramilitary organization known to be funded and backed by the Kremlin, has been named the group responsible for the disturbances along the Austrian and Swiss border. Several news agencies, including the BBC, have validated the reports of violence, but requests for confirmation from both nations have been met with silence. Bob, back to you."

Mal turned the volume down and looked up at the screen. Anya's name still wasn't listed. He walked over to the long row of windows and looked out at the snow-covered parking lot. Small fields of yellow illuminated the flat area where cars huddled under blankets of snow. He pulled his phone from his pocket, pushed the one key, and put the phone to his ear. "Standby, Sunset Operative Nineteen."

He didn't say a word.

"Authenticate Hate," Fury answered.

"Power. We're at the hospital. She's being

admitted to the ICU. Thanks for the federal intervention."

"Meh, Nolan owes me one. I got him out of a jam a couple of years back." Fury brushed off the comment. "Dr. Montrose is calling in to get the game plan for her care. We want someone within the organization monitoring her care."

"Why? She's nothing to you." Mal stared out the window as snow started to fall again.

Fury released a long breath. "She means something to you. Friend, lover, I don't care, so don't bore me with the details."

Mal chuckled. "You suck."

"I do, but I'm damn good at it." Fury's laugh was low like his. "Oscar Team will be there soon. Relinquish the hard drive to Hoss. He's the team leader. He'll get it to the people it's supposed to go to. They're en route to your location, so Oscar Team will intercept them and do the handoff. You don't need to deal with any of the fuckers in the CIA."

"Thank you."

"Also, we're getting you an apartment in the area. You'll need somewhere to sleep. I called Harbinger and told him to pack you a bag and bring it up to you. You'll have to buy anything you need until he gets there."

"Would you have him bring up a couple of other items for me? I don't feel comfortable being this far north without them." Malice rattled off what he wanted.

"That last one isn't for you, is it?" Fury chuckled.

"No, but I think it's important," Mal admitted. "She'll need it."

"Could take a hot minute for me to find something like that." Fury sighed.

"I have faith in you, O' Ancient One." Mal chuckled.

"Come down to the Rose, and I'll show you ancient," Fury challenged.

"No, sir. I'm so damn tired you could blow a smoke ring at me and drop me," Malice admitted.

"Rough mission," Fury added.

"If it weren't for Anya, it very well could have been my last. They were waiting for me."

"That'll never happen again."

"Good to know, but it shouldn't have happened in the first place."

"Don't I know it. I've expressed my thoughts on the issue to the highest people in the organization."

"I would have loved to be a fly on the wall for that. Do you need a debrief?" Procedure mandated he complete his debrief and then his Go/No Go evaluation.

Fury made a growling sound in his throat before saying, "You can confirm the target was eliminated?"

"I can." He watched the man's brain splatter against the wall.

"That's all that is necessary at this time. Other matters have taken precedence."

Mal nodded, even though Fury couldn't see him. "I saw a bit about it on the news channel."

"Only the tip of the iceberg," Fury said.

"I figured. Not much below the water needs to be known."

"Truth. And thanks to your woman, we were able to pivot. Take care of her, Mal. Call when you have a release date. I'll work on those issues we talked about before with her visa or citizenship, but right now, we have other things on the front burner."

"Whatever it takes," Mal started.

"As long as it takes," Fury finished and disconnected.

Mal pocketed his cell and glanced at the monitor. Her name was listed on the black background. He took a deep breath and walked to the door.

CHAPTER 14

*M*al stood up, stretching a bit but still holding Anya's hand. The nurses were polite and gave him a padded wheeled stool to sit on. He was told by the nurses there was a nice-looking FBI agent at the door, and he thanked them for the information. Anya hadn't opened her eyes. The nurses said she was sedated and probably wouldn't wake until tomorrow at the earliest. He rolled his shoulders and cracked his neck.

"Mr. Adams?"

Mal looked over his shoulder. "Yes?"

The lead nurse pointed toward the door he'd come in. "There are five guys out in the waiting room who said you're expecting them?"

"Thank you." He glanced down at Anya and stroked the back of her hand.

"We'll take good care of her for you." The nurse smiled at him.

He nodded and put her hand back down on the bed. He walked out of the unit and was met by Oscar Team.

"Mal? I'm Hoss, this is Ramp, Halo, Squirrel, and that guy by the door is Hoot." Each man nodded as he was introduced. "Fury said you have something for me to take to the alphabet people." Hoss glanced over at the FBI agent who was guarding the door. "No offense."

The agent chuckled. "None taken."

Malice slipped the hard drive out of his shirt pocket. "You're supposed to tell whoever you deliver this to that this makes my contact and them even."

Hoss snorted. "You know it never works that way."

"I do, but he had delusions." Malice shrugged.

"We brought you some food. Didn't know the last time you had a chance to eat."

Mal blinked at the huge white paper bag. "It's been a couple of days." He'd been so worried about

Anya that he hadn't left her side long enough to eat.

"Figured. Nothing fancy, but there's a little place right on the Bering Sea that makes a killer breakfast. Haven't had their takeout, but it is what it is." Hoss handed him the bag. "We'll be back as soon as we run this to its owners and pick up your keys to the place you'll be using. Get your stomach full and get back to your woman. Between us and the Fibbie standing over there, we got your six until they pull us. Let's roll," Hoss said the command in a conversational tone, and his team moved in a well-trained singular movement to the door.

Malice ate the food, offering the Fibbie at the door some of it because he wasn't sure how any one person could eat that much food. Well, except for maybe Ice. Ice ate all the fucking time.

"I'll be here until midnight, then we'll do a shift change. My name is Theo Miller. Dean Sinclair will be the other agent here."

"Sorry you're pulling door guard duty," Malice said as they both ate.

"Don't be. My boss was on the other side of this door about two years ago, and Guardian made sure he and his family were taken care of while the rest of us were out tracking down the bastard who put him there. This is us returning the favor."

* * *

A HAND LANDED on his shoulder, and Mal jumped from his stool. One of the nurses stepped back and held up her hands. "Sorry. I didn't want to wake you, Mr. Adams. You haven't slept since you've been here, but Theo just buzzed back to the nurses' station. You have a visitor in the waiting room."

Mal blinked and stretched. "Sorry for jumping up like that, and thank you."

"It's okay. We tread lightly when waking people up around here," the nurse said as she left.

He glanced down at the bed where he'd rested his head for just a second … over an hour ago. Damn, he was tired, but Anya's infection was fighting the medication they were giving her. Her doctors admitted they were tweaking the cocktail of drugs they were using to fight the spread of the tetanus. She'd been in the ICU for over twenty-four hours now without much improvement.

He bent down and kissed her forehead. It was something he'd started doing whenever he left her.

"Be strong, my little sniper," he whispered in Russian, then headed out to the waiting area.

Malice pulled the door open, and a smile spread across his face. "H, you son of a bitch. Damn glad to see you."

"Don't talk about my mom that way," Harbinger said as he made his way across the lobby. They hugged, and Harbinger pushed him away. "What the hell is with the bush on your face?"

Mal stroked his beard. "Haven't had time to shave lately. This is Theo. The night Fibbie is Dean. Theo, this is one of my coworkers. H."

"Good to meet you." The Fibbie offered his hand.

"And you," H said, shaking his hand. He turned back to Mal. "I brought clothes and a shaving kit. The bosses said Oscar Team picked up the keys to your apartment."

"Thanks, man. Yeah, Hoss was here yesterday, I think. They had to go. Their R&R time in the States was over. So, I have the key and the address, but I'm not leaving until she's awake and doing better."

"How is she?"

Mal sighed. "The meds weren't working the

way they wanted them to, so they're trying a different combination. Her fever has lowered, and her blood pressure is back to normal. She hasn't come around yet, but they said they gave her a sedative."

H made a head movement, and the two of them moved to the far corner of the lobby so they could talk without the Fibbie listening. "What's the story between the two of you?"

Mal looked out the window and crossed his arms. "Actually, there isn't much. Just this feeling I got here." He rubbed his chest. "She's an amazing woman, H. A dead-shot sniper who saw a way out of a no-win situation by helping the assassin sent to take out her boss. She saved my ass on a mission that could have been my last. She's strong and makes me laugh. I like her."

"Attractive?" H lifted an eyebrow.

Mal knew the guy was teasing. "Yes, so you can leave now."

They both laughed. H rubbed his jaw. "Is it true they knew you were coming?"

"That's what she said. Five days' notice, so that was right after I was notified."

"Fuck, man, I hope the bosses find and plug that hole. I'd be happy to be the one to do it."

"You and me both, brother," Mal agreed.

They stared out the window for a bit before H snapped his fingers. "Ice wanted me to tell you that Paris went on a date with some guy she used to know in California. He traveled to Virginia to see her. He thinks she's into the guy. He figured it would upset you, but I'm thinking, based on what I just heard, it doesn't matter to you."

"It matters." Mal frowned. "Paris is a good kid. She needs stability in her life. Did Ice check this dude out?"

H chuckled. "Mother Mal."

"Damn straight," Mal grumped. "But no, I told you before, there's nothing sexual there. Just another kid who needed someone to help them."

"And this one?" H nodded toward the ICU.

"She's different. I don't look at her as a kid." Mal could feel his face heating up. Thank God his beard covered his cheeks.

"I get it," Harbinger said. "Believe me, I get it."

Mal nodded. "Have you heard anything from that woman in Europe?"

"Since she cut me loose? Nope." H shook his head and rubbed the back of his neck. "I have no idea what went south there."

"Then maybe you should find out?" Mal

suggested. He held up his hand, stopping Harbinger's comment. "I know, I know … I don't have a leg to stand on here. My relationships have lasted about as long as it takes to get off, but if Anya were to just walk away from me or dump me after all this … I'd probably go insane trying to figure out the why of it."

"Have you two …" Harbinger lifted his eyebrows.

Mal shook his head. "There wasn't a time we weren't being tracked, surviving a storm, or she wasn't fighting this damn infection." He sighed. "Am I being a fucking dog for thinking about sex when she's in the ICU? I am, aren't I?" Mal pushed both hands through his hair.

"What? Hell no. Dude, you're looking to the future. That's what you should be doing at times like this. She'll get better, and the future is something you can work on together. You've never felt this way before. You're allowed to hope." Harbinger nudged him with his elbow. "I'm really glad you found someone you want to walk with forever, or hell, even for just a little bit. It's an amazing trip."

Mal sighed and looked at his friend. "Which is

why your ass needs to get back to Europe and find that woman."

H shrugged. "I'm still licking that wound. Maybe later, maybe never. Can I stay here and let you go to the apartment to clean up and shave that bush off your face?"

"Thanks, but I'm not leaving." He wouldn't until he could talk to Anya and see for himself she was getting better.

"Figured. Give me the key to your apartment and the address. I'll stow your bag, and I'm going to grab some sleep. Do you want me to bring you back some food?"

"Yeah, enough for me and the Fibbie? They've been pretty cool."

"Done. I'll call South and let everyone know you're alive." H took the key and listened as Mal rattled off the address.

"Hey, H, let Ice know about Anya, will you? Tell him Londyn and Paris should know, too."

H lifted a finger in a salute from the door. "Be back after I grab some shuteye."

Malice brushed his beard with his hand as he looked out the window. The snow had stopped, but the day was dark and gray as it was that time of the year that far north.

"Everything okay?" the Fibbie asked from his post by the door.

Mal jerked and turned back to him. "Yeah, just tired. I was staring out into nothing and just zoning."

"Been there, done that. How's she doing?" Theo asked.

"Seems to be doing better. Blood pressure is lower, and the fever is, too."

"I'm glad. Thanks for the intro, by the way. Most times, people treat us like we aren't here." Theo chuckled.

"Yeah, not the way I function." He had respect for most people. Unless they took advantage of children, then all bets were off. He headed back into the ICU to assume his post watching over a woman he barely knew and yet had become so damn important to him.

* * *

ANYA ACHED in a way she'd never ached before. Every muscle of her body screamed when she shifted in the bed. Her eyes were so damn heavy, but she managed to blink them open.

She focused on the pristine white walls, then

the bright fluorescent lights. She shifted again and groaned.

"Hey." Mal's face appeared over her. "You back with me?"

It took Anya a minute to translate the words in her head. "Where did I go?" She spoke in Russian. English was too hard at the moment.

"You were pretty sick and out of it for a while." Malice spoke in Russian and pushed her hair from her brow.

His touch felt so good. She turned into it instinctively and didn't care to try to figure out why. "The wound?"

"Yes, but you're going to be okay. The doctors said they think you'll make a full recovery."

"We are on the boat?" She moved again and immediately regretted it. The sound that came out of her was close to what a wounded animal would make.

Malice's face frowned. "No. Are you in pain?"

"No … yes, I hurt. My muscles are sore. What happened?"

"Do you remember getting into the life raft?"

Anya blinked. "No."

"Ah," Malice said. "We left the ship and were picked up by a helicopter. We're in Nome, Alaska."

"America?" Anya asked.

"Yes. That's right. We've been here for three days."

Anya felt his hand holding hers and looked down at the connection. "You stayed with me. You did not have to do this."

"I did. I wanted to be here for you."

She blinked several times, noticing the dark circles under his eyes and the lines that dug into his brow. "You need to sleep." She lifted her hand and touched his face. He smiled, which softened his intense gaze.

"I will now. I couldn't before."

"Why?"

"Because when you were sick, you asked me to not leave you." Malice shrugged, then added, "And because I care about you."

Anya stared up at the big man, understanding the power of those words to the protector in front of her. "That makes me special, does it not?"

Malice chuckled. "You've always been special, but it does mean you're special to me, yes."

"As a friend? Like those you told me about?" Anya spread her fingers and laced them with his.

"More than that if things work out." Malice

lifted her hand to his lips and kissed the back of it. "If I'm off base here, let me know."

"I do not know what that means." She liked the way his thumb moved over her skin as their hands remained linked.

Mal sat down, and she turned her head to look at him. "It means if you don't feel the same way, let me know."

"How do I know how you feel?" She smiled at him.

"You're feeling better, aren't you? Sassy woman."

Anya smiled wider. She liked his touch. No, she craved it. The man was a craving and she wanted to experience him. She wanted it badly. "I like the sound of more. Will your Guardian allow this?"

"They don't tell me who I can spend time with," Malice said.

"That is good." No matter what she wanted, her body was not on board. Yet. A wave of exhaustion swept over her. "Was it infection that did this to me?"

"Tetanus. The rusty knife."

Anya huffed. "Dima bringing more trouble from the grave."

"You'll have to stay at the hospital for a while.

Then work with doctors to ensure no long-term damage was done to your nerves."

Anya licked her lips. "I have no money to pay."

Malice smiled at her. "Guardian is paying, but even if they didn't, money isn't an issue. I have enough for anything you need."

"But that is yours." Anya frowned at him. "I will pay you back. I will pay Guardian." She could get a job. Manual labor if it was available. She could work. She closed her eyes and relaxed a bit. She could find a way to make money and pay them back.

"You already paid, Anya. You saved my ass, and you gave us information that kept Karl from completing his mission in Switzerland." Anya blinked and jerked her head toward him. She hissed at the jolt of pain the sudden movement caused. "I'm getting the nurse to give you something for the pain."

"No. Wait." She gripped his hand as tightly as she could. "He was stopped?"

"From what I've heard and seen on the news, yes," Malice said.

Anya felt sick to her stomach. "Was he captured?"

"I don't know, why?"

"He … he is dangerous." How did she detail the thousand little things the man had done that had warned her to run as fast as she could when she found out Dima was going to give her to Karl? She was willing to help an assassin to escape from that man. She killed Dima when he attacked her. That wasn't planned, but Dima made his choice when he tried to kill her. That was how desperate she'd been to get away from Karl. The man was *evil*. He killed because he *liked* it. His father condoned his viciousness and even applauded it. She'd seen him do vile things to people and kill or torture animals and laugh while he was doing it. "Can you find out if he was killed?" *Please, please let him be gone*. Anya begged whoever was in the heavens to let him be gone.

Malice nodded. "I can find out." He stood up again and leaned over her. "Anya, you don't need to worry about him. He doesn't know where you are, and why would he try to find you anyway?" He touched her chin, and she looked up at him. "I would never let him or anyone else hurt you. Never. You know what and who I am. You understand this promise?"

Anya sighed and shifted in the bed. The movement pulled a groan from her. "I do. Thank you.

You are probably right." She squeezed his hand. "I am making a big thing where there should not be anything."

Malice smiled down at her. "I'll get the nurse."

He left the room, and Anya closed her eyes. The differences between the man who had stayed by her side and Karl, who was supposed to be her future, were vast. The difference between darkness and light. How had she been so blessed? She opened her eyes and blinked back tears. "Babushka, I made it across the ice."

CHAPTER 15

*K*arl Rostova slammed his fist onto the table. "Who? Who was the traitorous son of a bitch who leaked our plans?"

His aide was the only man in the room who had the balls to answer. "Everyone at the compound is dead. If it was one of them, there is no way of knowing."

"Not true," Gusev, a man who'd been with him in camp and in Switzerland, said from the end of the table. "Dima's whore was not found."

Karl turned and stared at Gusev. "Repeat that."

"The marksman. She was gone." The man leaned forward. "Several of our men were killed by a large caliber weapon. She could have been aiding the assassin."

"Preposterous," another of his lieutenants said. "The whore had no access to communications. She could not have known what we knew."

Karl dropped down into his chair. "Dima was aware."

Gusev nodded. "He was there the night your father briefed us. He could have told her."

Karl turned his stare to Gusev. "Find that bitch."

Gusev nodded. "And when we do?"

"I will pull her heart out of her mouth and watch her choke on her own blood." Karl lifted his hand and made a gesture that cleared the room. He sat back in his chair and let the rage curl in his gut. That his father had died was not of a concern to him. The old man was only good for his connections, and even that influence was starting to wane. That his plans to become the highest-ranking military official in Russia had been thwarted *did* concern him. The plan was perfect. Now he owed money and blat for a failed mission. The whore would die. Slowly. Over weeks, perhaps. He'd experimented with others. The whore would suffer for what she'd done. She'd suffer, and he'd smile at each scream.

∗ ∗ ∗

JEWELL CONNECTED her system to Guardian's, and Con was up on her screen a moment later.

"Any problems?"

"No. Archangel cleared everything," Jewell said as she worked. "It wasn't hard to find. It was the worm. I'm cleaning and setting up our programs."

"Send me the—"

"File," Jewell completed. "Should be to you by now." She worked as Zane looked over her shoulder. Her husband was wearing a sidearm, had a gun in an ankle holster, and two knives she'd seen as they got ready that morning. He wasn't taking any chances, and neither was she. The chairman's people had been accepting but not happy about her bouncing around in their system and had given her a time limit. The chairman himself had pulled the head of his IT into his office and, while Jewell and Zane were present, insisted she had carte blanche over the systems but had agreed on a time restriction to keep the peace. She detected several systems snooping, but it wasn't difficult to block them and do her work.

"I have limited time in the system. You'll need to figure out who it was being transmitted through

173

or to," Jewell continued to type and glanced at the clock. "Come on. Work faster."

A hand landed on her shoulder. "No one is going to stop you. Do what you need to do to make everyone safe."

The reassurance flowed through her, and she worked like a woman possessed. When she hit the last upload, she glanced at the clock. "Fifteen minutes to spare."

"Check your work," Zane said from behind her. Jewell nodded and started a review of everything she'd done.

She was just about finished when Con's voice came through the speaker of her computer. "I've found where the information was going." Con's voice sounded ominous.

"Where?" Zane and Jewell asked at the same time.

"Sending it via encrypted message."

Jewell blinked. The connection they were talking on was secure. The extra precaution curled a fist around her gut. She accessed the program and ensured she keyed the encryption code on her end before securely opening the message.

"Shit," Zane said from behind her.

The message read: Congresswoman Ellen Harrier.

She turned around and mouthed to Zane. "She's dead."

He nodded. "Con, you need to send this up the line. We aren't in a position to do it."

"I copy. I'm signing off and running a few more programs to see what went out of that location and when. I'll forward it as soon as I have that data."

"I'll call in when I can talk," Jewell said before closing the connection to Con. She opened a note on her computer.

>>She died four months ago. Has a vote been held to replace her in her state?

Zane shook his head.

>> A staffer?

Zane looked at her and nodded imperceivably. "Are you done here?"

"Almost." Jewell deleted the note and finished her review of her work. She unhooked her computer from the host system and closed up shop. "Ready."

"We have more systems to get through and a fuckton of flight time in between each one." He picked up her computer bag and helped her up out of the chair. Jewell nodded. They would be gone for over two weeks, but securing every system was the only way they knew for sure each was clear. The thought of having one organization in charge of security was not going over well, but the preponderance of evidence showing the chairman's computer had been hacked couldn't be overlooked, especially by the chairman's own computer people, which was the reason she was finally allowed access.

* * *

CON SENT the information up the line and expected an immediate call, but two seconds was way faster than he'd anticipated. Plus, the call was being routed from a drop number he'd given the NSA. The name on the other end was even more surprising. His old boss's number. "Go."

"Con, you work for Guardian now, right?" Nate Thurman didn't beat around the bush about anything.

"You know I do."

"Listen up, I don't have much time, and if I get busted for this, you better find me a fucking job with Guardian."

"What do you have, Nate?"

"You have someone in Alaska? Someone who recently completed a job in Russia? And a woman? A Russian?"

"Dude, I don't have a clue." Con wasn't giving the man shit. His loyalty was one hundred percent on Guardian's side of the fence.

"Run this up your flagpole and get them to authenticate it. I intercepted it while I was working on another issue. The Rostova Group is hunting the woman and the American. The CIA can confirm it. You didn't hear it from me." The line went dead.

"Fuckity, fuck, fuck, *fuck*!" That meant he'd have to call Fury because he couldn't pass it off to Jewell and Zane. *Son of a bitch*. He hated the guy as much as the assassin hated him … which was something no one ever wanted. But whatever, the man was a child under all that growl and glower. Con took a deep breath. He could be an adult, and he needed to send this to the right person, which was Fury.

He punched the direct line to the Rose. "What the fuck do you want?" Joseph snarled.

"Nothing from you, asshole, but I have information from a highly placed person in the NSA that the Rostova Group is hunting the asset that was in Russia recently. The one that gave us the information that the computer system for the Council may have been compromised."

"Go on."

"Not much more than that. The group is hunting your asset and the woman. He said the CIA can confirm it."

"The Rose is clear." Fury disconnected the call. Con narrowed his eyes and glared at the phone. "You're welcome, asshat."

* * *

Fury hit the direct line to Tori's office.

"Hi, Joseph. It's—"

"Tori, I need you to work with your contacts." Joseph told her what Con had told him.

"Give me ten minutes." Tori hung up on him.

He looked at the phone and cracked his neck. "I'm getting really tired of that shit." He put the phone down, then picked it up again, dialing the number scratched on his notepad.

"Dr. Montrose."

"Lillian, I need you to get a medivac up to Nome, Alaska. We need to get them out of the area. Shit is going downhill."

"I'm on it. I haven't checked in today. Do you want me to call and initiate a discharge?"

"No. Not yet. I'll let you know when to do that. Get the aircraft sorted and call me back."

"I'm on it. Mercy Team Five is clear."

Joseph put the phone down, then spoke to the device. "That's how you end a conversation. It isn't that fucking hard, is it?"

"Are you talking to yourself?" Thanatos asked from the doorway.

"Yes, and beware, I'm going to answer myself, too." Fury leaned back in his chair. "We're going to have to medivac Malice and his woman out of Alaska."

"Harbinger is there, too. Make sure he exits with them." Thanatos came in and sat down in the chair across from Fury. "Why are we bringing them down? Has her condition worsened?"

"No. The Rostova Group is hunting them."

Thanatos stared at him. "That could be bad on multiple levels."

"Tell me about it." His phone rang, and he put it on speaker. He was in a secure location, and Thanatos was his second in charge. "What did they tell you?"

"They confirmed it. My contact also added that

Karl Rostova is blaming the woman for his father's death and the collapse of the Switzerland initiative."

"No shit." Fury rolled his eyes.

"They tortured and killed the indigenous people at the Rostova encampment."

"Fucking bastard," Fury said more to himself than the others.

"Too true, but it gets worse. He figured out how they got out of Russia. His people found their gear and weapons stashed on the outskirts of the town, along with two dead Rostova men. They tore the town apart after that. During that rampage, someone remembered the FSB officer vouching for someone they suspected on the docks. They boarded the ship and tied the FSB officer to the deck. It wasn't pretty. Their source told them that the FSB officer told them everything before they killed him. He told them Anya was so sick she couldn't walk without help. Joseph, they split him down the middle and wound his entrails around his neck." Tori sighed. "Get your people to safety. These guys are monsters."

"Working it. Thanks for the intel."

"I'm clear." Tori hung up.

He punched Con's number. "What?"

The computer operator hated him as much as Fury hated the keyboard warrior. Which was a perfect situation as far as he was concerned. "Where is Oscar Team?"

"Standby." He listened to the rapid tapping of keys before Con answered, "On a flight over the Pacific. Do you need me to divert them?"

Fury glanced at Thanatos. "No. The Rose is clear."

"Two assassins against a handful of Russians."

"Not fair odds. The Russians don't have a clue what they're inviting, but Malice's woman is sick and, therefore, a handicap."

Thanatos shrugged. "I still like their odds. Especially since this woman is a shooter."

"So do I." Fury picked up the phone. "I need to let Mal know what's going down."

"Dr. Montrose is on line two."

"You take it. I'm calling Mal." Joseph hit the button to the operator.

CHAPTER 16

*M*al walked back into the hospital. Anya had finally convinced him to go to the apartment and sleep in a bed. He got eight hours of solid sleep since Harbinger had volunteered to sit in the lobby of the waiting room with the Fibbie. Not that he didn't trust the Fibbie, but he knew Harbinger's capabilities.

Malice spent a half hour in the shower and hacked through his beard, shaving for the first time in over three weeks. He stopped by the small grocery store and got some chocolate and peanut butter candy bars for Anya. She wasn't eating much, so the nurses suggested some sweets might be welcomed. He also bought a stuffed polar bear for her. Because he was a sap. Thankfully, all of it was in a bag, so H couldn't give him too much shit.

"Well, that face I recognize," H said as he walked into the hospital. "Glad you hacked off that wild man thing you had going on."

Mal frowned. "Why aren't you upstairs?"

"Because they moved her to a regular room. The doctors are with her, and the Fibbie is watching. I didn't want you to head upstairs and freak when she wasn't there. I'll take you to her. She's nice, by the way."

"You visited with her?" Mal was shocked that the nursing staff had let him in.

"She was moved last night, right after you left." H turned around and walked backward as they talked. "She made me promise I wouldn't call you. She insisted you needed to sleep. I happened to agree with her."

Malice glared at his friend. "You aren't supposed to pick sides."

"Ha! That's where you're wrong, and that woman is a-fucking-mazing." Mal spun and walked beside him. "Her English is better than mine."

"That's not hard," Mal grunted.

"Stop being a dick. I like her. I can see why you

two hit it off. She won't let you mother her, you know. I figure she could kick your ass when she's healthy. Definitely outshoot you." H stopped in his tracks. "Dude, Val is going to have someone she can hang out with who actually understands the business."

Malice groaned. "Val is a bad influence."

"The hell she is." Harbinger laughed. "Damn, another natural-speaking Russian in the group. It's a good thing we all speak the language."

"Another?" Mal glanced at Harbinger.

"Yeah, Smith. He's Russian."

Mal frowned. "How the hell did I not know this?"

"You weren't involved in the mission in Russia." H looked around and lowered his voice. "Smith is a morbid fuck when it comes to sending a message. I'll tell you about it sometime. That's where I met Oscar Team."

"Ah, right. The Mongolian horse adventure. I remember you telling me about that."

"Dude, if I never ride a horse again, it'll be too soon," H groaned. "Here we are. She's in the room Theo's guarding. Go figure." H laughed. "Fess up the keys. I'm going to go to sleep and get something to eat. Not necessarily in that order."

Mal tossed the keys to him. "Truck is in the front lot."

"Perfect. Call me if you need me." H did an about-face and left the way they'd come. Mal shook Theo's hand before he entered the private room. "This is much nicer than the ICU ward."

Anya smiled at him. "You shaved? You are very handsome, with or without a beard. I like both."

Malice rubbed his chin. "I'm glad you approve."

"Very much." She laid back against the pillows. "I told your friend to not call. You needed sleep."

"I should have been told."

"Why?" She smiled tiredly.

"Because you're important to me." Mal could feel his cheeks heat up. Damn it, never before had he felt like a twelve-year-old kid when talking to a woman. Everything with Anya was different.

She lifted her hand, and he took it. "It has been a long time since I have been important to anyone, but I agree with you. You are important to me, too. This is why I insisted he let you sleep. This room is nice. It is so big and all for me. The doctor says three more days, maybe four, and then physical therapy. He said I don't have to stay here to do that. Can we go to Virginia?" She moved over a bit so he could sit on the bed with her. She didn't wince in pain anymore when she moved, which was a huge improvement.

"Absolutely. You'll like it there. I brought you something."

"You did?" she asked. "What is it?"

All of a sudden, he felt rather stupid for the impulse buy, but … *fuck it*. "It isn't much, just something to brighten your hospital room." He pulled the bear out of the bag.

"Oh!" Anya exclaimed and reached out to take the plush animal. Her hands shook as she held it. "For me?" She glanced at him as if the bear was a mink coat or a diamond necklace before she slipped back into Russian and asked again, "Really? For me?"

"Yes." Mal smiled at her. She pulled it in, examined its big blue eyes, and ran her fingers through its plush fur. She kissed its black nose, then hugged it.

"Thank you." She opened her arm, holding the bear with the other, and he leaned in. The peck on the lips he intended to give her morphed when she held onto him and chased the kiss. Mal sealed his lips against hers and moved up the bed, wrapping her in his arms. She sighed into their kiss. Mal let the kiss linger before pulling away, regretting every centimeter of space between them but knowing it wasn't the place or time to start anything. Still ... "Wow."

Anya opened her eyes. "Yes. Wow." She leaned into him. He ran his hand up and down her back. "I should leave the hospital now. You will check me out and take me home to your bed."

He chuckled. "We can wait."

"You can wait. I don't want to." She sassed back at him as he held her in his arms. God, the sensation was complete heaven. Anya fit against him perfectly.

"I don't like it either, but I'm not going to risk you getting sick again."

Anya leaned back in his arms, still clinging to the stuffed bear. "Have you ever heard of sex making a person sick?"

Mal blinked. "Well, no ..."

Anya's eyebrows lifted. "Well, then, I think I should leave now."

"When you're cleared by the doctor." Mal dropped his forehead to hers.

"You are not fun," Anya grumped.

"I promise to try harder when you get out."

She let out a husky laugh and slid her hand between his legs. "Harder?"

Mal groaned and grabbed her hand. His cock went from interested to diamond hard at her touch. Fuck, he *was* twelve when he was around her. "Woman, you are trouble, aren't you?"

"Yes. But you knew this from the start." Anya laughed.

"I did," Mal agreed. "I brought you something else." He grabbed the bag. "Try one of these."

Anya looked at the candy bar and opened it. "Try it," Mal coaxed. His phone vibrated in his pocket. He stood and took it out as Anya slid a cup out into her hand. "Trust me, it's good. I need to answer this."

She waved him away as she took a tiny bite of the confection. He laughed when her eyes went wide. "Oh." Anya licked her lips and took a bigger bite. Her eyes rolled backward, and she made nummy sounds.

Malice put the phone to his ear and walked out of the room. "Go."

"Authenticate Hate." Fury's voice snapped across the connection.

"Power. What's up?"

"Are you somewhere you can talk freely?"

"Hold on." Mal walked to a small visiting area.

"I'm not in a secure location, but there isn't anyone around."

"There's a situation you need to be aware of. Karl Rostova has launched an all-out search for Anya."

"What? How do you know that?"

"We have our sources. Intel told us that members of Rostova's inner circle have rounded up the locals who were at the camp you destroyed and tortured them. The only thing they were asking about was their sharpshooter and an American. They tore the town of Tiksi apart and found your stashed gear and her rifle. You didn't mention the two dead men from Rostova's group."

"Shit. It was them or us." Malice glanced in the direction of Anya's room. "Damn good thing he has no idea where we are."

"That's where you're wrong. Renat was also tortured and killed. Rostova put the boat and your exit together. The CIA had a secondary informant on the communications ship where Renat was posted who reported the information. Renat told Rostova Anya was sick, and you had to help her to the raft and that he put you in international waters near Alaska before they slit him from throat to cock and wrapped his neck with his intestines."

Mal digested that information. "He wouldn't come here. Hell, he wouldn't know where to look."

"What name did you register her under at the hospital, Mal?" Joseph asked.

"Fuck, it's in the computer system."

"Exactly. He knows where you are. Oscar Team is halfway to Mongolia, and I don't have anyone closer. Where's Harbinger?"

"He just went back to the apartment to grab some sleep. He was here last night while I slept."

"I have Dr. Montrose calling to send a medivac plane to Nome. You have about four hours before we can get there and get refueled."

"Any intel on personnel movement?" Mal kept an eye down the hall. Theo glanced down at him and then did a double take when Mal shook his head slowly. Theo stood away from the wall and moved his jacket away from his weapon. He was a damn sharp cop.

"Not yet. We've just got this information, so we're behind the power curve."

"It would be better to take her to the apartment. Now. It's obscured by Guardian, correct?" Mal hated the exposure of the hospital, and multiple routes of entry and exit precluded a secure sanctuary in the middle of the hospital. Then there was collateral damage. The patients and staff at the hospital could be caught in the crossfire. "We're sitting ducks here."

"Excellent idea. Get her ready to go. I'll inform Dr. Montrose of what's happening, and we'll dispatch her on the aircraft with the appropriate meds. You'll go to South Dakota to the Annex for Anya's rehab. No one will find her there."

Mal cussed. "I'm moving her. But, Fury, I'm thinking of another idea."

"What's that?"

"The mission in Juba, South Sedan. The exit strategy."

Fury was quiet for a long moment. "Do you trust her that much?"

"With my life."

"That may very well be the price," Fury said.

"It's the best way."

"Can she make it?"

"H will ensure it."

"You're the bait?"

"I am."

"Do it and keep your phone on. I'll get rid of the local cops and make sure the flight plan is filed with big red letters."

"Copy, I'm clear." He disconnected and hit up H.

"Dude, I just got into bed."

"Get back here, stat. We have to move her. There's a threat. Bring the go bags and the special item you brought up with you."

"Plan of action?" He could hear H moving in the background.

"Exit strategy similar to Juba."

"I'm the bait."

"No, you're with Anya. I'm the bait. You'll make sure she's ready and makes it onto that airplane."

H cussed. "I don't like it."

"I don't care. My op, and you're wasting time."

"En route," H said and hung up.

He motioned for Theo to come down the hall. The man jogged down to him.

"We have a legitimate threat. H is coming back and we're disappearing."

Theo nodded. "What do you need from us?"

Malice thought for a minute. "Get me some scrubs for her. She can't wear a hospital johnnie when I take her out of here." He pulled his wallet out of his back pocket and grabbed a stack of one-hundred-dollar bills. "Buy her some shoes and someone's coat, too. A hat to cover her blonde hair."

"Got it." Theo took the money and jogged down the hall. Malice was right behind him.

"These are so good." Anya had three empty wrappers on her lap when he walked in. She smiled up at him, but the smile slid off her face immediately. "What's wrong?"

"Rostova. We're leaving. I'll explain later."

Anya's color faded immediately. "What?"

"They may already be here." Malice pulled her blanket back. A nurse raced into the room. "I just got the call from the doctor. I'll take out the IV port. We're getting her prescriptions ready. A wheelchair is on its way."

Anya gripped that stupid bear as the woman took the IV out of her arm. As soon as she was free, Anya stood up. Mal grabbed her arm and steadied her. "I need shoes." Anya looked up at him.

"I have them." Theo came into the room. "The nurses wouldn't take your money. Clothes from a gym bag. Tennis shoes they can replace. They should be good enough to get you out of here." The pile of clothes was dropped onto the bed along with his cash. Theo was out the door as quickly as he came in.

"Do you need help?" the nurse asked her.

Anya nodded. "Please."

Malice went to the window in Anya's room, turning his back to the women while keeping an eye on the door. He shut the blinds, giving Anya a sense of privacy but not leaving the room. He wouldn't risk it. The hair on his arms stood up. He lifted his jeans and pulled his weapon from his ankle holster.

"Ready," Anya said from behind him. He turned around and blinked. Wearing leggings, tennis shoes, and an oversized hoodie, she looked like she was maybe seventeen years old and was coming or going to the gym.

"Let's go."

"Wait." Anya stopped him. "My bear." She turned carefully. The nurse rushed back to the bed and grabbed the toy. "Here. Good luck."

"Thank you," Anya said to her.

Another nurse ran down the hall with a Ziplock bag of medicine plopped in the seat of a wheelchair. "Instructions are on the bottles. If you have any questions, call us."

"Let's go." He helped Anya into the wheelchair

and started pushing her. He pulled his phone out of his pocket and hit the speed dial. As soon as it connected, he directed, "H, pull up in the back, by the dumpsters."

"I'm at the hospital now."

"We'll be there in three." Mal snapped the phone shut.

"Mal." Theo jogged down the hall. "Here." He extended a white knit hat with a huge white tassel at the top. Anya put the medicines and her bear down as Mal continued to push the chair. She put the cap on and shoved her hair inside.

"Agent Sailor told me to go with you if you need me." Theo had his coat with him.

Mal got it, he did, but he couldn't risk another life. The gun Theo had wouldn't make a bit of difference if Mal and Harbinger didn't know where he was or what he could do. He extended his hand. "Theo, thanks, but it's better if H and I handle this alone. We've worked together for years." Theo grabbed his hand for a firm shake as Mal kept them moving to the rear of the hospital. Theo hoofed it down the hall with them. "If you need anything, just call."

Mal nodded. "Be careful. These men are vicious motherfuckers."

"The nurses have been told to say you were discharged earlier today."

"That won't stop them from questioning the staff. Beef up the police presence here and around the hospital." Mal reached the back door by the cafeteria and pinned his new friend with a stare. "Theo, don't underestimate these men."

"I understand. Be safe."

"You, too," Mal said as he helped Anya out of the chair. "Ready?"

"I am." She nodded and held onto that damn white bear. "Let's go."

CHAPTER 17

*H*arbinger drove straight to the airport. They pulled over, and Mal jumped out of the truck. He pulled his go bag out of the bed of the truck before leaning into the cab. He kissed Anya firmly on the lips. "Listen to H, and for God's sake, don't miss."

Anya's mind twisted like a pretzel trying to understand what was happening. "Do not miss? I have no rifle."

Mal smiled and winked at her, then turned to H. "H, we're setting this up the same way. Wait until they show their hand. Don't jump the gun."

"Fuck you, asshole. You jumped first last time." H pointed at him. "Do not get yourself killed."

"Not the plan, and I always follow the plan."

"No, you do not."

"The hell you do," Anya spoke at the same time as H.

Mal laughed. "I'll see you soon."

Anya grabbed his hand. "This is a promise. Do not break it." Her future was with this man. She couldn't explain how she knew it, but she did. The certainty of the fact etched itself in her very existence.

"This is a promise, and I will do everything in my power to keep it." Malice squeezed her hand. "H knows the plan." Malice kissed her again and nodded to H. Anya watched as he jogged toward the terminal with the bag slung over his shoulder.

A stream of cars drove by them from the terminal area. H mumbled, "Fury did his job."

"Which was?" Anya asked as they drove past the terminal and onto the far side of the flight line.

"Remove all civilians. I'm dropping you off here. Just hunker down. I'm going to ditch the truck and make my way back here. Don't fucking shoot me, okay?"

"I repeat for those with bad hearing. I do not have a gun and cannot move faster than an old dog on a cold night." She wasn't happy with not knowing the plan.

"Right ... about that." H pulled off the road again. Then he jogged around the truck and opened the door. "Do you need help?"

"No." She probably did, but she wouldn't admit it. Anya clambered ungracefully out of the truck's cab and hung onto the vehicle's door. H pulled out two big bags and dropped them into a ditch filled with snow. Then he lifted out two gun cases. He held up the black one. "This is the same make and model as the rifle you had to leave. Malice made sure I had it with me before I came up. I'll move all the heavy stuff. Hunker down here and stay out of sight. I'll come back for you, and we'll take up our position."

"For what?"

"Wiping those bastards off the face of the earth." H winked at her and held out his hand. "That culvert will keep you and the bags from sight. It'll be colder than a witch's tit in a brass bra, but we've got cold-weather gear in the bags. Can you put it on without help?"

Anya lifted an eyebrow. "You are descriptive. I can manage." She hoped. As it was, she was exhausted and shaking, but if Malice and his friend needed her to help, she would.

H helped her down the bank and threw the

bags into the cement tube he'd called a culvert. It was a word she didn't know, but it looked like a drainage tube. She leaned back against the freezing cement. "The bag closest to you is yours. I'll be back."

She nodded and waited for him to leave before she grimaced and moved toward the bag. She pulled out a parka and put it on, sitting on the tail end. The pants took longer to get on. She pulled them up to her thighs, then rolled on her hands and knees to move the waist of the pants up before sitting back down. She was sweating from the effort. Calming herself, she concentrated on breathing in and out. When she was able, she opened her eyes and pulled the boots out of the bag. She replaced the ill-fitting tennis shoes, and her feet were immediately warmer. Anya picked up her bear and wiped off some dirty snow from his feet. She placed him carefully in the bag, then inched her way to her rifle.

The gun case was new, but the rifle was not. There were scratches and mars on the wooden stock, but the action was pristine as she withdrew the bolt of the firing mechanism. Her hand caressed the metal, and she dry-fired the weapon several times, getting a feel for the pull of the trigger. It took more pressure than her weapon. That was a mental note she'd register. Anya pulled one of the silver blanket pouches out of the bag and spread it on the ground before she took a position on her belly and propped the weapon on her bag. The scope was not in the right place. She carefully loosened the bolts and moved it a fraction of an inch closer. She laid her cheek against the stock again and focused on the scope. The wind was nonexistent. Her first shot would also be her calibration. Hopefully, H's rifle in the second case was zeroed in and ready for action.

She heard the runner before she saw him. Snow had started to fall, and the wind had picked up a bit. She angled the rifle toward the sound and had H in her sights as he crested the ridge to the north of the runway. He jogged to her and crawled in the tight space.

"Give me a second." He took no time to put on his cold-weather gear and remove his weapon. It was different. An American version of a sharpshooter's rifle. He put his hood up and looked at her. "I found a location for us. It has direct sight to the private plane ramp."

Anya nodded and held the groan in as she worked her way out of the cement drainage area.

She couldn't remember the American name. H helped her up the ditch and carried both weapons and his bag as they moved into position. The wind accelerated, blowing the snow sideways, but the American clothes and boots were snug and warm.

Anya moved as quickly as she could but had to stop twice and sink to her knees. "I will be okay," she volunteered even though H hadn't asked. He waited until she could move forward and then helped her up.

They scaled a small knoll. A natural plateau on the far side would serve as their firing platform. H put down several of the silver sheets and then drove metal posts around them. She kneeled as he worked. A dappled white tarp was tied to the upper portion of the stakes. H crawled in, pulling his bag and both of their weapons.

"Do you want a tripod or …?"

"Tripod," she said and watched him pull two out of his bag. "I am not at zero."

"You have the skill," H said as he placed his weapon in the holder.

She did the same, then dropped her head down to rest her muscles. She knew her physical limitations, and she'd pushed past them on the walk to this place. "Let me know when I need to get ready."

"I will. Rest." She felt his hand on her back as he patted her fluffy coat.

"The plan is Malice will draw them out to the private ramp. They'll want to know where you are. We wait for his signal when they're out of the vehicle."

She nodded, her head still down, and her muscles relaxed. "What is the signal?"

"Usually someone dying," H said, then chuckled. "You'll know."

The wind howled, but the small depression and the tarp over them kept them from suffering the wind. Anya looked up and sighted her scope. "Where?"

"The largest hangar." She'd made shots in that type of environment, but with her weapon that had been sighted in.

Anya studied the target. "Five hundred and sixty yards."

"Five eighty," H said.

Anya frowned and reassessed the distance. "Five sixty." She was positive about her scope and her ability to assess the distance.

H didn't say anything but adjusted his weapon. She asked, "Wind?"

H lifted the handheld telemetry and waited a

moment before he spoke, "Fifteen knots out of the north, northwest."

Anya figured out the calculation and adjusted her sight picture. She dropped her head down to her hands again and closed her eyes.

A hand on her shoulder woke her. "Game time." She blinked and jerked up. "It's all right. Malice has moved into position. That means he's got intel that the bogies are inbound."

Anya had never heard the word bogies before, but she understood the context. She wiped her eyes with her fingers and assumed her position. She found Malice in front of the largest hangar.

The noise from a plane punctuated the sound of the wind. "Okay, when you see him move, take out as many as fast as you can. Miss Malice, if you can."

"I can, but I would rather not shoot in his direction until I know how this fires." Anya adjusted slightly and wrapped her finger around the trigger. Slightly more pressure. The first target away from Malice to judge the weapon. "You take the ones closest to him. I do not know this weapon."

"Great. You know he'll never let me live it down if I hit him."

"I will kill you if you hit him. That should be more worrisome." Anya lifted from the stock of her rifle and looked at H.

The man smiled at her. "Yep. You're going to fit just fine."

She frowned at him and returned her attention to the scope and the kill zone in front of her. "Wind?"

CHAPTER 18

*M*alice drove an airport vehicle he'd hotwired out to the private hangars and then parked in front of the largest hangar, which was currently vacant.

"In position." He checked his weapons prior to getting into the old airport SUV.

"Three callers have contacted the hospital, all calling different numbers but asking for Anya Baranov," Fury said.

Malice glanced over the terrain and wondered where Anya and H had set up. The weather had turned, and a front was moving in. "They gave the correct information?"

"According to the Fibbie you left there, yes. She was being transferred to a hospital in the lower forty-eight, and due to HIPPA, they couldn't disclose the location of the transfer."

"Enough information to get them off their asses." Malice could see down the road to the airport. "I have two vehicles inbound."

"Does H have comms with us?"

"No. He was on a transfer, not a mission," Mal said as he held up the binoculars to his eyes.

"Not a fucking excuse," Fury grated out.

"Says the man who did all his missions during the Stone Age." Malice could see two in each vehicle. "I count four."

"It's a team. Should be at least five," Fury mused.

"Yeah." Malice dropped the binoculars and started a scan of the area. "All are coded?"

"In defense of yourself and others," Fury confirmed. One of the credos they'd signed on to was the use of deadly force when directed or in the defense of self or others. "Of course, if you leave someone alive, we'd be more than willing to find out what they know."

"Roger." If someone survived, they'd be extremely lucky. Malice saw movement across the runway. "Third vehicle." He lifted the binoculars and homed in on the cab of the vehicle. "Two more."

"Only six. You have two assassins and a sharp-shooter."

"I'm not worried about the odds."

Fury snorted out a laugh. "I fucking hope not."

"Do you have a wife?" Malice asked as he watched the plane Guardian had sent for them fly past. The rumor was the beautiful redheaded doctor at the Rose was his wife, but no one had confirmed it. Someone had also said she was what the training facility was named after. Again, conjecture and rumors.

"Why do you ask?" Fury responded.

"Curious how you make it work."

"We can talk about logistics later. Focus on your mission."

"My mission is protecting her. Believe me, I'm focused. I'm getting out of the vehicle now. They're about a minute away."

"Copy. Don't die."

"Whatever it takes," Malice replied. It was a fatalistic view of things, but he'd do what it took to make sure Anya was free from that fucker Karl.

"Yeah, but dying isn't what it takes for this, asshole." Fury's response was immediate. The comms went quiet after that, and Mal didn't question Fury. He didn't want to die, but there was always a chance in his line of work.

Malice got out of the truck and looked in the direction he believed H and Anya would set up. He clapped his hands together several times before he signed. *Three vehicles. Take out left and right. I have the middle.*

He waited for several seconds and then repeated the message. Before the cars merged on his location, he leaned against the hood of the vehicle and signed the message again.

When the trucks stopped in front of him, he waved at the driver of the first vehicle, the one in the middle of the group. The men dismounted the vehicles, and Malice took note of the weapons not so cleverly concealed in the bulk of their winter clothes. "Hey, you waiting for the transport? They're having an issue with their hydraulics. Happens in this weather."

"Where are the passengers?" one of the men asked in very rough English.

"You aren't from around here, are you?" Mal asked.

The man shifted and glanced at his partner before he growled, "The passengers?"

"I don't know, man. I'm just here to help park the plane." Mal shrugged. "Why do you want to know?"

The man who spoke English turned to the man beside him and began speaking in Russian. "He says he doesn't know."

"Kill him."

Malice dropped into a modified squat as he pulled his automatic. His movements were fluid and practiced. The gun leveled, and the target acquired. Without conscious thought, he triple-tapped the first man. Three in the chest before he dropped to his side while shifting to the second target.

A warm spray hit his face as he acquired the second target. Malice pulled the trigger as soon as his sight picture was aligned. Men on the sides of him dropped as he filled the fucker that had ordered his death with lead.

Malice rolled and leveled his gun, searching for another target. There were none standing. He lifted to his knees, his gun trained on one body, then the next. The men on his right were shot through the chest. Blood pools congealed close to the bodies. The men on his left were a different story. Neither had faces. The large caliber bullets of a marksman's rifle had entered the back of their heads and blown off the front of their skulls. He stood and glanced down at his jacket and jeans. Hair, bone, brain, and blood spattering clung to the material.

"Are you alive?" Fury's voice drawled over the comms.

"Yep, and they're dead."

"So, no hope of an interview?"

"Not unless you head to hell and catch up with them." Malice glanced back and saw where H and Anya were now standing.

"Not in my travel plans."

"Yeah, mine either." Mal drew a deep breath. "Are the Fibbies handling cleanup?"

"They don't know it yet, but yes." Fury chuckled. "I've told the plane to land. They're doing a hot stop, will load you up, and then head south. You'll stop in Spokane to refuel, pick up Dr. Montrose, then head to the Annex in South Dakota. You'll stay there until Anya is recovered and her clearance issues are resolved."

"Are there problems?" He watched as Harbinger helped Anya up the embankment behind them. She leaned into him heavily. Fuck, he wanted to be there to help her. Hell, he'd carry her.

Why the hell wasn't H doing that? Well, for one, Mal would probably rip H to shreds for holding his woman.

"Dude, are you there?" Fury asked.

"Sorry, what? Gunshots are ringing in my ears." *Yeah, right.*

"I said not anything we can't handle. Take the downtime and get her acquainted with life in the States. Remember, if we find out she's a plant, she's your responsibility and your problem."

"She isn't a plant."

"I hope for your sake she isn't," Fury said, almost as if he was talking to himself.

"The plane is on final. I can see the landing lights."

"H and the woman?"

"Getting back to the vehicle. They'll be here shortly." He hoped. He wanted to put his hands and eyes on her to ensure she was okay.

"Tell H to contact Anubis when he lands at the Annex. Anya is not to be allowed in any of the classified areas. As far as she knows, the hospital is the only thing there. Copy?"

"I do, and I'm not stupid." He rolled his eyes so hard he could see his brains.

"I never said you were, but women make men crazy." Fury sighed.

"You say that like you know a thing or two." Malice chuckled and let out a breath as he saw the truck H was driving move around the airfield.

"I do. My wife was the person who saved me from walking into oblivion. If this woman is the one for you, make sure you can trust her. Having that link is essential."

"She's saved my ass twice now." He looked over at the headshots. He'd bet his annual salary that Anya was the one who took those shots. Harbinger was damn good. He'd wager Anya was better. "The plane is landing. Thanks for the assist on this."

"Whatever it takes," Fury replied.

"As long as it takes," Malice finished for him as he watched the plane touch down and immediately reverse its engines. By the time the plane taxied to where he was waiting, Harbinger was driving up.

Malice went to the passenger side door and opened it before the truck came to a full stop. "Are you okay?" Black circles that hadn't been there earlier lined the bottom of her eyes. She leaned against the back of the seat and didn't move when he touched her face with his fingers.

Anya finally nodded. "Tired. Weak. But okay, I think." She turned to him. "You are a mess."

Harbinger laughed. "Always."

Malice glanced over at his friend. "Fuck you."

"Nah, I'm particular, and you aren't my type," H joked and put the vehicle in park. "I'll get the guns and bags."

"No!" Anya jumped and sat up.

Malice pivoted, palming his automatic. He scanned the area. "What's wrong?" he asked as he looked for a target.

"My bear is in my bag. I want it."

"Holy fuck." Harbinger placed his hands, one of which held a weapon against the dash. "We need to work on your communication there, lady."

Malice dropped his head back and stared at the gray sky and the snow floating down from the heavens. "I'll get the bear, but for the love of my sanity, don't do that again. Especially right after something like this." He lifted his head and motioned to the six dead bodies freezing on the tarmac.

He retrieved the little stuffed animal and gave it to her before he lifted her off the seat and carried her to the steps that had just been lowered from the G6 aircraft.

"Wait, I want to see them. I want to see if one was Karl Rostova." Anya pointed at the dead bodies. Mal walked over so she could see the men he killed. "This one was the man who ordered me killed."

Anya shook her head. "I do not know this one." She looked at the other bodies. "I do not know any of them. Your rifle is off center, but the shot was good."

"The headshots were yours?" Mal asked.

"Yes, you went low, so I went high. Is this not the way you do things?" She leaned against him, and her body went limp in his arms.

"Works perfectly for me." Mal adjusted her in his arms, walked up the stairs, and put her in one of the large leather recliners. "There's a shower in the back and clothes in the storage area. Something should fit you."

The pilot's face said more than his words did. Malice glanced down again. "Thanks. I'll hit it as soon as we lift off."

"Sounds like a plan." The pilot went back to the door and moved out of the way as Harbinger came up the steps. "I take it the gentlemen on the tarmac aren't coming?"

"No, they declined the invitation," Malice said and buckled in as Harbinger did the same.

"Good to know." The pilot pulled the door shut and headed back to the flight deck. The plane was moving seconds later and took off within a minute of the door closing.

Mal popped off his seat belt as soon as the flight crew turned off the seat belt sign. He knelt in front of Anya. Her eyes were closed. "Can I get you anything before I clean up?"

Her eyelashes fluttered open, and she mumbled, "No, just sleep."

"Okay." He hit the buttons on the recliner, and her chair extended. Anya turned on her side and closed her eyes. He ran his hand down her hair and stared at her. A hand on his shoulder startled him.

"She'll be okay. Go get cleaned up, and then we'll get some food."

"Right." Mal stood up. "Fury said we're flying to Spokane, and that's where the doctor's coming aboard." He started to walk toward the rear of the plane. H put a hand on his arm, stopping him just past the kitchen area. "She did well out there, but it took a lot out of her. She fell asleep as soon as she put her head down. I woke her up when you moved into position."

"She's been through a lot. We're going to the Annex so she can recuperate in peace. Oh, Fury wants you to contact Anubis as soon as you get there." Mal nodded to Anya. "She can't know about the Annex."

"Well, no shit." Harbinger huffed out a laugh. "As it is, she knows too much about you."

Mal frowned at his friend. "That couldn't be helped. She knew I was sent to kill Rostova and saved my ass from a trap. Denying what I'd come there to do after I blew that camp to hell was off the table."

"Dude, I wasn't judging. I want her to be with you. She's snarky as hell and will put you in your place when you need it." H moved over to the refrigerator and opened it. "Want some water?"

"Yeah, but the shower type. Will you go through the storage areas and see if you can find me some clothes?"

"Will do. If not, we can brush most of the body parts off those." H pulled out a bottle of water. "Then I'm going to sleep for a couple of hours. You interrupted that, remember?"

"Not my fault," Malice said as he went into the bathroom and took off his clothes. He hung his coat on the back of the door. He'd wipe the mess off it after he showered. The boots he could clean off and the socks were fine, but the jeans went into the pile he'd shove into a garbage bag and get rid of at the Annex.

He'd just stepped his ass into the shower when Harbinger walked in. "Dude, they have a clothes setup the same way they do at the safehouses. I got your size, and I'll shove these into a garbage bag."

"Thanks, man." Malice dumped a load of shampoo into his hand. "Maybe I should transfer my moniker to you. Momma H."

H looked up at him from where he was stooped over, picking up bloody clothes. "Do that, and I'll have to kill you. Speaking of which, your woman threatened to kill me today."

Malice had shampoo streaming down into his eyes, but he scraped at the suds so he could see H. "Say what, now?"

"I said something about the fact that I hoped I didn't hit you with my shots. She wanted the ones farther away from you because she wasn't certain of the rifle."

"And?" Malice swiped at the shampoo again.

"And she said if I shot you, she'd kill me. Matter of fact. No threats, no hysteria, just stone-cold truth. Have I told you that I *really* like this woman?" H stood up with a tight bundle of clothes in his fist and waggled his eyebrows at Malice.

"Stay away from her, or I'll kill you." Malice may have growled that warning.

"Ha! See, you two were meant to be together." H laughed again as he left the bathroom.

"Fucker," Malice grumbled as he finished lathering up. The thought that Anya had threatened an assassin with as many kills as Harbinger was kind of funny. She was a spitfire. He never really knew what would be coming out of her mouth. He chuckled as he rinsed the soap out of his hair and off his body.

It took him no time to dry off and dress. He checked on Anya, who hadn't moved. H had found the couch and was stretched out, too. He opened his eyes and pointed to the kitchen. "Food in the refrigerator. I'm checking out if you got the watch."

"Sleep. I'm solid."

Harbinger closed his eyes and turned toward the back of the couch. Malice grabbed water from the fridge and sat down next to Anya. He stared at her as she slept, which was ... well, creepy as hell, but fuck if he could stop. He was all kinds of messed up inside because of the woman. Feelings he'd never really experienced had poked their head to the surface since he'd met her. Attraction he'd felt before. Lust was another he was acquainted with. But he'd never felt the fear he'd known when she went into those fucking seizures when they were on the rescue raft. He protected those who couldn't protect themselves, but the overwhelming necessity to ensure her safety was far beyond anything he'd experienced. The need to make sure she was guarded, healthy, and that she was … *his* … God, it was so fucking foreign to him. And the kicker was the woman was as deadly as he was. She didn't need his protection. But fuck it, that *wasn't* the point.

The sensations tangled up and lived in the pit of his gut, twisting and turning until he didn't know which way was up. Was that what people called love? Was love an explosive and frantic feeling of not being enough? Did love mess up your mind until you weren't sure if what you were feeling was real or something you'd made up? Hell, they hadn't even had sex yet, and the idea of losing her had his stomach tied in bonds that were soaked in water and tightened to the point that he had no idea how to release himself from the feeling.

And *that* was the crux of the situation, wasn't it? He didn't want to free himself. He was a willing prisoner. He extended the chair he was sitting in and turned on his side, so he was facing the woman who had turned his world on its head.

"You stare too loud," Anya said without opening her eyes.

"Is this a dream?" Malice said the words that were on his mind. If it was, he didn't want to wake up.

"No. This is life." She opened her eyes and gazed across the space that divided their two chairs. "Although I am afraid that one day you will wake up and not want to be with me."

Malice frowned. "Why would you say that?"

"I am nothing. I have nothing. As much as I hate to speak it, *I am less*." A tear formed in the corner of her eye and slid down her nose, dripping onto her hand.

"You will never be less with me." Malice reached over and wiped the trail of the tear with his finger.

"You say this now. It is what you believe now. Who knows what you will believe in a year?" Anya shrugged.

Malice lifted to make sure H was still sleeping.

When he was sure he was, he lowered back down and spoke so only she could hear him. "I've never had these feelings before. The burning in my gut of worry for you. The need to protect and take care of you." He held up a hand when she started to speak. "I know you don't need that, but it's what I want to do. I want to relieve you of the burden of being so strong for so long. I want to carry you so you can rest. I want to have a relationship that is so warm it will ease the cold that has filled your life since your babushka died. I want all of that and more. More between us when you are healthy." Malice sighed and shook his head. "I'm horrible with words."

Anya smiled as another tear fell. "No, your words are beautiful. I like what you want. I want it, too." Her eyes closed for a moment before she opened them again with effort. "I must sleep. Stay with me?"

"Sleep. I'll be here." Malice watched as she lost her battle to stay awake and fell into slumber. He turned and looked up at the roof of the aircraft. He'd stay with her until the end of time if God would allow it.

CHAPTER 19

*A*nya jerked awake when the plane touched down. Malice was sitting next to her, and Harbinger was lying on the couch. "Where are we?"

"Spokane, Washington. The state. We're taking on more fuel, and the doctor is coming aboard."

Anya sat up, and Mal messed with the buttons on the side of her chair that folded it back together. She blinked and looked at the inside of the plane. It wasn't like the pictures she'd seen of airplanes. She'd never flown in anything but a helicopter. The opulence was unmistakable. "This is very nice."

"It is. We don't usually get to travel in such

comfort." Malice chuckled. "I think one of the big bosses loaned us his private jet."

Her eyes darted to the leather seats and appointments of brushed gold. Was it real? She touched the cold stone of the table beside her. A faint gray line traveled through the white stone. She'd never seen such beauty. "Rostova has not this wealth," she whispered, tracing the gray line on the table with her finger. And she thought Rostova was extremely wealthy.

"Most people don't."

A door at the front of the cabin opened, and a man in a flight suit went to the door and opened it. He exited right before a woman came up the stairs.

"Hi, I'm Dr. Lillian Montrose. You can call me Lilly. I take it you're Anya?"

Anya blinked at the vibrant woman with a wide smile and red cheeks from the cold. The coat, scarf, and hat the doctor wore were expensive and lined. Her boots had heels that would cause Anya to break an ankle. Her purse, gloves, and boots all matched. The woman looked as if she had walked out of a magazine. Her dark chestnut-colored hair flowed around her shoulders in curls that fell in thick layers. A sudden and overwhelming feeling of inadequacy crushed Anya's sense of self-worth.

If that woman was typical of Americans, why would Malice be interested in her? She was *nothing* like her. She nodded slowly and said, "I am Anya Baranov."

Malice stood up and extended his hand. "Dr. Montrose. I'm Mal. Thanks for coming with us and for your help when we were being evacuated out of that life raft."

Lilly shook his hand. "That diagnosis was a stab in the dark. But all the symptoms pointed me in the right direction. As fortune would have it, I'm heading to South Dakota for my rotation at the clinic where Anya will be cared for. Normally, I'm on a Mercy team. My teammate is taking the next four months off. He's getting married, going on his honeymoon, and then setting up house, so it was a perfect time for me to supplement the staff at the clinic." Lilly came across the plane to Anya. "How are you feeling?"

"Tired and I ache." Her throat was sore, and she was feeling feverish, too, but she didn't want to complain.

"Okay. Where are the meds the hospital released her with?" The doctor looked at Malice.

"Shit." He rubbed his face. "In the truck?" He looked at H.

"Yeah." H nodded. "I threw them in the glove box when I was stashing the truck, and we fucking forgot them."

The doctor lifted a single eyebrow and stared from Mal to H. "Well, it's good I brought my medical kit with me." She pointed at Mal. "Please go down to the ramp and grab the burgundy leather bag. Thanks." She turned to Anya. "Let's go to the back of the plane. I'm going to get your vitals and call back to the hospital to see what they gave you."

Anya frowned. "I am fine here. They did not do anything wrong."

"Who? The doctors?" Lilly asked, and Anya could see the confusion in her expression.

"No, Mal and H," Anya said, stilling Mal's departure. "When people are trying to kill you, medicine is not a consideration."

Lilly smiled at her. "I wasn't being judgmental. I work with Guardian. I understand the situations that some of our people get into. I just want to make you're comfortable and make sure you're looked after." The doctor narrowed her eyes as she stared at Anya. "You look flushed. May I?"

Anya nodded, and the doctor put the back of

her hand on her forehead. "You feel a little warm. Mal, would you please get that case for me?"

"Absolutely." Malice ducked out the door and was gone.

"I really think we should go to the back of the plane. I'd like to do a quick exam. We can come back out front after if you feel up to it." Lilly stood up. "I'll help you back."

Anya grabbed the doctor's arm and stood up. Her body shook with the effort. Malice was back and ducking through the door. "Here it is."

"Could you bring it back?" the doctor asked as Anya steadied herself.

"How about you bring the bag, and I help Anya." Malice set the bag down, and Anya gave a small yelp when he swung her into his arms.

"Well, that's one way of doing things." The doctor chuckled.

Malice looked at her. "When did the fever start?"

Anya sighed and leaned her head against his shoulder. "When I was sleeping. I did not have it before." She swallowed hard. "My throat is sore, too."

Malice dropped a kiss on her forehead. "Let the doctor take care of you. I'll be right outside the door if you need me." After he sat her down on the side of the bed, Anya looked around. What type of money did it take to own a plane with a bedroom?

Malice backed out, and the doctor came in. "Okay. So, can you tell me exactly what's going on?"

"Going on?" Anya stared up at the woman. "I do not feel well. Could you please use simple English? I don't understand some sayings."

"Oh, damn, sorry." The doctor knelt beside her. "Tell me how you feel."

"Hot, my throat is sore, I'm exhausted, and I ache. Not as bad as when I first woke up at the hospital, but close."

"And they'd just moved you out of ICU when you had to leave the hospital? Can we take off this coat for a minute?"

Anya nodded as the doctor helped her take off her cold-weather gear. She started shivering the second the coat came off. The doctor did her exam and had Anya lie down on the bed. "Okay, before I give you anything, I'm going to call back to the hospital in Nome and get the medications you were taking and what they gave you. I'll be right back."

The doctor opened the door to the bedroom,

running into Malice. "Oh, hey. You can go in. I'm going to call her doctors."

Mal waited for the doctor to leave before entering. "I feel like shit for forgetting your meds."

"I forgot, too. This is not something you wear."

Mal's eyebrows popped up. "You mean not something I own?"

Anya scrunched up her face. "You do not keep? Yes? English is not easy."

"It isn't." Mal kneeled beside the bed and pushed her hair away from her face. "The doctor will take care of you, and when we get to South Dakota, you'll get stronger. I'll take care of everything. You don't have to fight, hide, or worry."

Anya closed her eyes and tried to smile. "I like this idea."

* * *

SOUTH DAKOTA WAS NOT MUCH different from Siberia. Anya looked out the window. The cattle were not caribou, and the herders were not nomads, but the land … It was so similar. The cold, white winter and bright blue skies reminded her of the days she'd spent growing up. A knock at her door turned her head.

"How are you feeling this afternoon?" Dr. Montrose asked.

"Much better. I do not need a hospital bed." Anya wanted to leave as soon as she'd arrived, but Malice and the doctor decided against her wishes. And if she would let herself admit it, she was in rough shape. But now, four days later, she felt almost human.

Lilly chuckled. "And today, I may agree with that comment. Let me take a look at your charts first." The doctor opened a laptop computer that stayed in the room with her. Anya caught a glimpse of movement out her window. She smiled as Malice jogged toward the clinic.

"Oh, I see what really makes you feel good," Lilly said from the other side of the room.

"He does," Anya admitted, feeling her face heat with embarrassment.

"Well, everything here looks good. If you promise to not do anything too strenuous, I'll discharge you today. I think Malice has arranged a place for you to stay while you're doing rehab. The damage to your legs from the seizures will eventually get better, but physical therapy will speed that recovery."

"I will do the work. I want to be over this." She

was sick and tired of being sick and tired. "Why did the tetanus affect my legs and not my arms?" She was glad it hadn't, or she wouldn't have been able to make the shots she'd made. Sometimes, her legs screamed with pain or twitched uncontrollably. Her arms did not.

"That is the mystery of the human body. I can't tell you, but I can get you rehabbed with one of our best physical therapists." Lilly smiled at Malice as he walked in. "Did you bring her clothes?"

"I did. Just as you asked." He held up the bag in his hand.

"You knew?" Anya's jaw dropped. "You knew I would be out today and said nothing?"

Mal had the decency to look caught in his little deception. "I didn't know for sure. The doctor said maybe."

Anya rolled her eyes. "You sound like a child caught in the …" She said the Russian equivalent of cookie jar.

"Who me?" Malice pointed to himself. "Never."

"Phfft …" Anya made a noise, shook her head, and laughed.

"I believe I said a strong possibility." It was Lilly's turn to laugh when Anya's eyes popped open, and she crossed her arms while staring at Malice.

The doctor chuckled. "Oh, I think you've met your match in this one, Mal."

"I believe you may be correct, doc." Malice laughed and put the bag on the bed.

"Okay, I'll go get your meds and some muscle relaxers for any flare-ups in your legs. Only take them if you can't work through the pain. You're still on antibiotics, after many courses of antibiotics, so any birth control you may have been taking is completely useless." The doctor looked over at Mal. "That will be your responsibility until she's off the meds."

Anya's eyes went wide, and Mal flushed a vivid red. The doctor did a double take. "Damn, that was an assumption on my part. When we talked about … Sorry if I assumed something …"

"It is all right." Anya felt heat rise to her cheeks, too. "It is something we want, but as of yet, it has not happened."

"Oh, well … Then, as your physician, I would encourage you both to take it easy, at least for the next month or so. After that, your body will tell you what you can do."

Anya's jaw dropped. "We must wait for a

month?" She turned to Malice and, in Russian, said, "I do not care what she says. I am not waiting a month."

"I don't know what you just said, but I said to take it easy. That's not the same as no sex." Lilly looked from Malice to Anya. "She just said she wasn't going to listen to me, didn't she?"

"Maybe?" Malice's face was red from embarrassment, and he was fighting hard to not laugh.

Anya squinted her eyes at him. A man-child. But he was a gorgeous man-child.

"Let me go get the medications. Anya, do you need help getting dressed?"

"Malice will be here," Anya replied and took a little bit of joy out of watching the deeper shade of red appear on her assassin's face.

"Then I'll be back when I have the paperwork and meds." Lilly walked out of the room and closed the door after her.

Anya cocked her head and blinked at Mal. "Did I embarrass you?"

"Yes, and you're the only one who can. That should tell you something." Malice opened the bag he brought. "Mike White Cloud's wife is about your size. She sent over some clothes. Her name is Tatyana." Malice looked at her.

"She is Russian?"

"She is," Malice acknowledged. "She wants to meet you, but I asked her to wait until we were settled in the cottage."

"Cottage?"

"There's a small Drover's cottage. One room, but it's snug and enough for us. It was either that or we would be staying as house guests." Malice glanced at her. "In separate rooms."

"This, I do not want." Anya sent him a determined glare. "You, I want."

Malice stopped pulling clothes out of the bag. "I want you more." His voice was low and filled with grit.

The tenor of need went through her and resulted in a full-body shiver. "Then help me dress so we can go to this cottage."

CHAPTER 20

*M*alice walked slowly, helping Anya as she moved across the uneven ground. He'd already been to the cottage. A quick trip to the grocery store in Hollister filled the shelves with food, although there was a dining facility for Guardian members. Anya couldn't know about that yet. Of course, she could see the buildings, but she didn't inquire, and he didn't offer the information.

He used a truck Mike White Cloud had given him when he'd arrived, so the short walk from the clinic to the truck and the truck to the cottage wouldn't be too taxing for Anya. Lilly had warned him repeatedly to not let Anya do too much the first couple of days. He took the doctor's word as gospel.

"Here we are." Malice opened the door, turned on the light, and helped her into the small cottage. He shut the door and watched her expression.

She gazed around the small room, then smiled at him. "It is perfect. And warm." She walked over to the table and brushed her fingers over the tabletop as she stared at the bed. "Do you think it will hold both of us?"

Malice walked up behind her and put his hands on her shoulders. "Maybe we should find out."

Anya turned to look at him. "I would like that very much."

"But …" Malice leveled a stare at her. "We're going to go slow and easy. I don't want you back in the hospital."

Anya unzipped the cold-weather coat she'd arrived at the ranch with and let it drop from her shoulders to the floor. "No hospital. Slow."

Malice bent down for a kiss. "And easy."

"So easy," Anya replied before her lips hit his.

Malice broke the kiss and moved them over to the bed. She slipped out of her tennis shoes, stood next to the bed, then stared up at him. "Your move." He sat down on the bed and unfastened her shirt slowly, kissing the freshly bared skin as he progressed. Her body was tight and athletic. Finding scars with his lips, he traced them with his tongue. She slipped out of the shirt and unfastened her bra. Malice watched as she dropped the lace material in front of her. The deep purple scar of the knife wound blazed a trail across her skin, ending at the swell of her breast. He started there, tracing the scar and kissing the path.

Her hands landed on his shoulders when he captured the hard nub of her breast in his mouth. She mumbled encouragement in Russian. Like he needed the pep talk. Damn, he was hungry for her. Only it wasn't a surface hunger. It was an ache that echoed through his entire being. He wasn't sure who unfastened her jeans, but they fell from her hips, and she stepped out of them.

His fingers slid off her panties, and he leaned back to finally see the beautiful woman who had mesmerized him so completely. Anya wasn't shy. She reached for his shirt, and he lifted his arms, drawing the material off.

"God in heaven," she said in Russian as she ran her hand down his chest and abs. His muscles jumped under her soft touch. "You are so big." She looked up at him. "Show me more."

There was no need to ask him twice. Malice stood up, keeping his eyes on the woman before him. Her athletic build tripped every trigger he had and a few he didn't know existed. The way she looked at him had him wanting to climb the Empire State Building and beat his chest with pride. Pure lust filled him as he toed out of his boots and lost his jeans and briefs. His cock slapped his stomach before he grabbed it in his fist.

Anya put her hand on his and moved his hand from his cock. She wrapped her fingers around his shaft, and he jerked in response to her touch. "This is mine." She looked up at him. "Yes?"

"God, yes." His hands found purchase on her shoulders. "Yours." She stroked him several times, and his thighs shook as he fought the urge to throw her on the bed and bury himself inside her.

"Make me feel beautiful."

Her words pulled him from the haze he'd fallen under. His hands lifted to her face, and he stared at her. "How can you not feel beautiful? When I look at you, I see nothing but beauty and strength. I am so lucky to have found you. To me, you are exquisite. Not even the greatest masters could create an equal to the beauty I see in you."

He leaned down and swept her off her feet. Turning, he carefully laid her on the bed and moved over her. "Never doubt that you're beautiful. Never doubt that you're mine."

He lowered and kissed her softly, trying to express the emotion he couldn't put into words. She shifted, and he moved between her legs. He lifted from the kiss they shared to look down at her. As he entered her tight, hot core, he stared at the woman he held. Anya's blue eyes held his, and the moment was fucking magical. There was no other word for it. He lowered for another kiss and moved slowly in and out of her. He knew in his heart she was his destiny. He would cherish and protect her for the rest of his life.

Anya arched under him. "More." The word was whispered, but it was a command, and he responded immediately. He went deeper and a bit harder. Her fingers dug into his back as he kissed her again. Anya broke the kiss and arched, her head pushing back into the pillow as her body tightened around his cock. There was nothing he could do. He exploded as her body rippled around his cock.

He held himself up on both elbows. Barely. He let his head rest on her shoulder and reveled in the feel of her hands traveling up and down his back. "Holy hell." He shuddered as he pulled out of her.

"I agree," she said in Russian. "That was magnificent."

He nodded his head, still catching his breath. He jerked his head up. "Fuck. Protection. I didn't wear a condom."

She patted his cheek, then dropped her hand onto the bed. "I know. We can worry, or we can make sure we use protection going forward. I choose to not worry."

Malice groaned and dropped to his side, pulling her with him. "You make me crazy. I lose my mind when I'm with you, but I should have protected you."

"We are both adults. I forgot, too." She was silent for a moment. "Is it wrong that I like making you lose your mind?" She snuggled next to him with her head on his shoulder.

"No." He fucking loved what she did to him. How much she affected who and what he was when he was with her. He'd never had that type of relationship. Never had the emotions, the need, or the desire to be integral in someone else's life. And yet, with Anya, he had all of it. He closed his eyes. He wouldn't have it any other way.

ANYA WOKE to Malice's kisses on her shoulders. She always slept on her stomach and must have moved into that position as they slept. She sighed heavily and let out a small moan as his hard cock pressed against her leg. "Protection," she muttered.

"Already in place," he whispered as he moved her hair and kissed her neck. The sensation sent little shivers through her and heated her core, where they all settled and seemed to intensify. Malice spread her legs with his knee. She kept her eyes closed and moved to accommodate his hips. He kissed the rim of her ear, then licked it. Those little shivers turned into lightning bolts. She gasped, and he made a sound of complete male satisfaction.

His arms slid up along her sides and under her hands. She wound her fingers through his as he entered her. The position was something she'd never imagined. He covered head to toe, and she relished the intimacy of the union. She couldn't move. She was completely vulnerable to him, and it was pure bliss.

Anya's body was his. She had no fear, no concern, and no hesitation with Mal. The past blurred when she was with him, and her future beckoned her. Her future was with Malice. She knew it with a certainty that scared her. Yet it didn't stop her from moving forward or falling for the rugged American who blushed like a schoolboy.

She gasped when he returned to her ear. All thoughts dissolved immediately as she melted under his tongue. His skin held their combined heat, and his fingers tightened around hers. She lifted her head and arched her back. The subtle change of position ignited the explosion building deep inside her. She arched harder, and he lifted a bit, thrusting deeper. She squeezed his fingers and yelled his name as she came. The tightening snapped, sending heat from her sex through her body. She dropped to the mattress as Malice finished. He rested his head on her shoulder. "Fucking amazing."

She nodded. Yes, it was amazing. Wonderful in ways she'd never experienced. She'd fallen hard for him and prayed fervently he felt the same way about her. But she wouldn't be needy. She wouldn't ask or force the conversation. It would come in its own time, or it wouldn't. Life had a way of working out. Her babushka had always said that. Anya held onto those words. *Please, please let it work out.*

CHAPTER 21

*M*alice dropped to the floor and pounded out pushups. The twins were trying to kick his ass, but he was younger than they were and stronger. He'd started training with them and Mike every morning before he went back to the cottage and either took Anya to PT or worked with her on her exercises. They'd fallen into a routine that was comfortable and satisfying. She refused to let him cook for them after he made her his fried peanut butter and jelly sandwich. He was pleasantly impressed he didn't burn them, and she actually ate them. But she cooked the next meal and every one since then. He considered that a win for both of them. After over a month of damn good food, he needed the workouts to keep in shape and keep the weight off.

"Mal, phone!" Mike called to him from across the gym floor.

"Be right there." Mal jumped up and rolled his shoulders. "Thanks, guys, see you tomorrow."

"Any—"

"Time." The twins said one word each as they pumped out pushups in unison. It was freaky how they did that.

Mal picked up the phone that Mike had left off the hook. "Malice."

"You son of a bitch. You've been here for over a month, damn near two as a matter of fact, and I find out from Harbinger *after* he goes back to Virginia?"

"Hey, Reaper. There were a few complications with my last assignment."

"So I heard," Reaper drawled. "I understand one of them is a five-foot-nothing blonde Russian. What happened to Londyn's sister?"

"Harbinger has a big mouth, and I was never involved with Paris. For one, she was too young, and for another, she was pregnant. Besides, according to Ice, she's met a good guy." Malice grumped, but the smile that spread across his face when he thought of Anya displayed itself in full force. Paris wasn't even a dim footnote in his brain at that point.

"She had a girl, by the way. Harmony received some pictures from Londyn a while back. And we had a boy. Carter. He's my clone, or that's what Harmony says."

"Congratulations, man, I didn't know she was due so soon. When did that happen?"

"She went about a month early, but everything ended up okay. Carter is six weeks old now. Thank God Maggie is living with us full-time. I'd forgotten about the sleepless nights and around-the-clock feedings. She's a godsend."

"Maggie? That's your country doctor friend from back east?"

"Yep. We finally convinced her to come out and live with us. But I digress. What's up with you? I thought you and Paris were a thing. How come I thought that?"

"I don't know. Maybe there was a longing for a relationship you sensed, but when I found the real thing, I never looked back. Thanks for letting me know about Paris. Anya and I'll send them some-thing." Malice was going to take Anya to Hollister, and they could see what they could find for Paris and also Reaper and Harmony.

"Anya, is that her name?"

"It is."

"So, it's serious?" Reaper asked.

"As a fucking widow-maker heart attack. I'm all in."

"Has she been cleared?"

Malice sighed. "No, not yet. Fury says it looks good, and the clearance should be coming through any day, but we'll stay here until all the paperwork is signed and she's legal."

"Good idea. Why don't we meet up this weekend for dinner? I'd like to have you out to the house, but until Anya has been cleared …"

"I get it. Yeah, we'd like that. It can't be anything too fancy. We don't have the clothes for that, man. I came straight off a mission, and so did she. Get my drift?"

"I do. Jeans are the standard in this area of the world, so the dress code isn't an issue. The last time I saw a suit out here, it was in a picture of a wedding in the *Rapid City Journal*. There's a steakhouse in Spearfish that's good. Saturday at, say, six? That'll get you back before midnight, or you could stay at a hotel and drive back in the morning."

"A hotel sounds best. That way, Anya can see some of the area before we come back up. Can you make any recommendations?"

Reaper gave him the name of a couple of hotels in the town and then told him the name of the steakhouse. "Oh, and you're buying, asshole."

Malice didn't care who picked up the tab but had to ask, "What? Why?"

"Because you didn't call and check in. I thought we were a team, man."

"Dude, tell me how wrapped up in the team you were when you found Harmony?"

"More than you could possibly know, my man. I had both Harbinger and Phoenix in tow. They fucking came through for us."

That surprised him. "You'll have to tell me about that sometime."

"I will. Speaking of H, how's he doing? He didn't talk much other than throwing you under the bus, which I'm sure was to divert my attention from him."

"No doubt. He's getting better."

"From what?"

"Oh, fuck. Man, don't say shit about it, but he

was engaged when he was hanging out in Europe. The woman decided to give him back his ring."

"Ooph …" Reaper grunted like he'd been punched and then said some cuss words that Malice was sure he hadn't heard before. And that was saying something. "Well, at least he dodged that bullet."

"Right? Doesn't mean shit to him at the moment, I'm sure. But I'm keeping an eye on him."

"Good ol' Momma Mal."

Mal chuckled. "Someone has to watch out for all you assholes."

"Truth. See you Saturday," Reaper said.

"Whatever it takes, my friend."

"For as long as it takes," Reaper finished, and the connection ended.

Mal gathered his gear and made the trek over the hill to the ranch side of the complex. He frowned at the vehicle outside the cottage. It was one he didn't recognize. Quickening his pace, he opened the door and almost knocked Anya on her ass. "Sorry." He grabbed her arm and steadied her. He saw Taty in the kitchen with a mug in her hand.

"Hey, is that your truck?"

Taty nodded. "I don't drive much, but I was heading to Hollister and thought I'd ask Anya if she'd like to go." Taty spoke in Russian as the women did when they were together. They both knew slightly different dialects of the language, but not enough to matter, especially because Taty was a linguist and adjusted without hesitation.

"I told her I have PT this morning." Anya sighed. "I would like to visit the town."

"I'll take you this afternoon. My friend Ice's sister-in-law had a baby girl, and my friend R … ah, Roman's wife, had a baby boy, so I thought we could look for something for them while we were in town. A present." Malice was glad he caught himself before he said Reaper's call sign. He'd been damn good about not giving Anya any more information about the people he worked with. Not that he thought she was a threat, but because it was required until she had her clearance.

"Oh, this is good," Taty said and took the last drink from her mug. "She needs to see something more than this ranch."

"We're going to Spearfish this weekend to have dinner with my friends Roman and Harmony," Mal said as he sat in one of the bistro table chairs. Anya walked over and sat on his leg. "If you think you'd like that?"

"I would very much." Anya smiled radiantly.

Taty nodded. "Good. You will like the area, and his friends are good people." Taty put her cup in the sink. "Do you still want me to pick up the groceries you needed?"

"No, thank you. I will do it." Anya looked at him for agreement. He nodded and winked at her. She blushed a bit and stood up as Taty walked to the door. Malice smiled at the effortless way she moved. The PT had helped her balance and nerve pain immensely.

Anya opened the door for Taty, and they spoke briefly before she shut the door. "We are going out to eat. Is it far?"

"Roman called this morning while I was working out. I came back to tell you he asked us to come down." He pulled her into him. "We'll go out for dinner, have some wine, some good food, and then stay the night at a hotel and come back the next day."

Anya frowned, which wasn't what he expected. "I have no money." She tipped her head back. "I must find a job. Taty has a job."

"You don't need to worry about money." Malice dropped a kiss on her nose.

"This is not funny." Anya reverted back to Russian.

The smile on his face instantly vanished. "I didn't say it was funny."

She pulled away. "I have been thinking about this. If I am to stay here in America, I will need a job, but what can I do? Nothing? I have no skill. No school. I cannot read English." She held up a finger and said, "Well, maybe a little, which is not good enough," in Russian.

Malice sat back down and watched as she paced and muttered to herself. When she stopped and looked at him, he asked in Russian, "May I speak now?"

Anya narrowed her eyes. "If you do not make fun of my worries, yes."

"First, I have enough money for both of us." He lifted his hand, stilling her objection before she said it. "We are together. You and I are with each other. Am I correct?"

"Yes, of course." Anya put her hands on her hips. "But this is not fair to you."

He continued as if she hadn't spoken, "Then what I have is yours. When we get back to Virginia, you can look for employment if that's something you want to do. If you *want* to. There is no need for you to stress about that at this point in time. I am not in a relationship with you because of your money or lack of it. I'm with you because I love you, Anya. There is no fair, and there is no stress. There is only us."

Her hands went to her lips, and he frowned. Why …

"You love me?" Her words were barely a whisper.

He stood and walked over to her. She tipped her head back to look at him. "It can only be love. Don't you feel it, too?"

She laid her shaking hands on his chest. "I do. It scares me so much. It is so strong and too soon. I don't want it to stop, but I am afraid it will."

He pulled her against him and held her tight. "I'm fucking terrified, too." Anya started laughing, and so did he. "We're a tough lot of killers, aren't we?"

She nodded. "Afraid of emotion, but not of war or death. We are silly, yes?"

"Yes, we are. I do love you, Anya. Never doubt that."

"And if your Guardian does not allow me to stay in America?" Tears formed in her eyes. "If they do not work the papers?"

"Then I'll go to Russia or any other country you want to live in."

"And they would let you come with me?" The worry in her eyes told him so much about the fears she *hadn't* been expressing.

Malice put his hand under her chin and stared at her. "You are worried about this?"

She nodded against his fingers. "And so many other things."

"Ah, my little one. You needn't worry. Your paperwork is going fine. I haven't said anything because you hadn't mentioned it. It should come through any day."

Anya blinked at him and then hit him with her fist on his shoulder.

He jumped. "Ouch!"

She stomped her foot and yelled in Russian, "You deserved that! You *must* have known I was worried."

"How? I can't read your mind!" Malice yelled back in Russian and rubbed his shoulder. "You have to tell me these things. I'm a *guy*. Guys don't understand women unless women tell us what to think. Geesh."

Anya blinked and then broke into laughter. "You want me to tell you what to think?"

"That's not what I meant." It *was* what he said, though. Malice frowned at her. "Just don't assume

I know what you're thinking about because, nine times out of ten, I'm going to get that wrong."

"I think maybe ten times out of ten." Anya leaned forward and kissed his shoulder where she'd hit him. "Should I kiss this again to make it better?"

Malice glanced at the clock. "You'll be late for your PT appointment."

"They can wait." Anya lifted his t-shirt and ran her fingers up his abs. His body reacted instantly to her touch. His shirt was off, and he was backing her toward the bed. To hell with going to PT. He'd figure out some excuse to use.

CHAPTER 22

*A*nya stared at the menu and willed her brain to understand the words written on the heavy card stock. She'd learned to *speak* English. To read it was a substantial effort. Harmony, who she met about ten minutes ago, leaned across the booth's table and asked, "What are you going to have?"

Anya lifted her eyes from the menu and answered honestly, "I do not know." That was an understatement. English lettering was so different from Russian letters.

Harmony laughed. "There are so many menu items, but I can recommend the petite fillet. It's amazing. Of course, I'm having a baked potato with piles of butter and sour cream." Harmony sighed. "I couldn't eat potatoes when I was pregnant with our son, Carter. The thought of it made me gag. But at least I didn't gain fifty pounds with him like I did Iris."

"You're beautiful at any weight or size." Roman, her husband, covered her hand with his.

"And you're lying, but I'll allow it." Harmony leaned into him and kissed him.

Harmony laughed when he chased her lips for several smaller kisses. She put her hand on his chest and turned to Anya. "And thank you again for the baby quilt. I love it." Roman caught her again and kissed her through Harmony's giggles.

Mal nudged her leg with his knee. "Need any help with the menu?"

She felt her shoulders lower as relief flooded over her. "Yes, please."

"Steak, fish, or poultry?" Malice put his arm around her shoulders, and she leaned into him.

She glanced over at the two across the table. They were laughing and talking between themselves. She whispered to Malice, "I would like fish." She loved cooking in the little cottage they shared, and while they had plenty of food, fish was not as abundant as it was in Russia.

"Okay, they have a trout dish. It comes with a

pilaf, which is different types of rice, and a side of seasonal vegetables, although I'm not sure what's in season at the beginning of March."

"I will try this." Anya smiled up at him. "Thank you."

He dropped for a kiss, and Anya savored the feeling of being cherished and protected. Malice was her shield from the unknown, and so much in America was unknown to her. Perhaps if she'd grown up in a city instead of the Siberian countryside, she would feel more in tune with the flow of life in America, but that was a supposition she couldn't support with facts.

The waiter took their order, and Anya listened as the old friends laughed and talked. She was included in the conversations, but the familiarity between the friends was something special to watch. Hopefully, one day, she'd have that kind of connection with the people Malice considered special enough to befriend.

She felt Malice's phone vibrate in his pocket. He removed his arm from her shoulders and answered it. "Go." He looked at her. "When?" She cocked her head and stared at him. "That's good. Yep. We'll do that. What? Is that the only limfac? Perfect. Thanks. As long as it takes." He put the phone down on the table. "That was Fury. He said your paperwork was signed this afternoon. As soon as Lilly clears you, we can head to Virginia."

She felt her skin tingle and form into goose flesh as the excitement of Mal's words registered. "Really?"

He put his arm around her shoulders again and dropped a hard kiss on her lips. "Really," he said when he lifted his head. "You don't have a clearance yet, which could take years, but your citizenship papers are complete. You're officially an American."

"Congratulations." Roman lifted the wine glass in front of him. "To Mal and Anya. May your journey be free from worry, filled with love, and blessed with an abundance of joy."

"What is limfac?" Anya asked after she took a sip of her wine.

"Limiting factor. You don't have a clearance, and it could take a couple of years for you to get one, as there isn't any emergent reason to hurry it along. But the majority of the people in this country don't have clearances. It won't be a problem for us." Malice raised his glass again. "To all of us. A bright future with the people we love."

He kissed her before they lifted their glasses and sipped the wine.

She had been waiting for this day, but … "Now I am worried." She laughed. "I know things here. What to do. Well, not here, but at the ranch. At the cottage."

Harmony reached over and put her hand over Anya's. "There's no need to worry. I have an idea. Roman said both of you came here straight from a mission. Would you like to go shopping for clothes and some personal items before you go back to Virginia? I need to buy some new clothes and a few things anyway. We can go to Rapid City tomorrow, and the guys can come along as our bag holders."

Anya bit her lip. She had no money, and as much as Mal had protested, she couldn't …

"She'd love to. Right now, she's worried about not having any money, but once we go around that topic a couple of times in private, she'll want to go shopping." Mal tried to suppress a smile. Anya poked him in the ribs, and he laughed, catching her finger. "Stop, you know I'm right."

"Maybe, but you did not have to say it in front of everyone," Anya chastised him a little bit.

"Oh, man, I so understand where you're

coming from, Anya," Harmony said. "When Roman and I were growing up, our families were dirt poor. He left our little town, but we found each other again years later. I was in a tight spot. I mean, I had nothing. Absolutely nothing, and I was in a huge mess of trouble of my own making. It's so hard when you've struggled to manage for so long, and you try just to exist." Harmony teared up a bit but continued, "But, Anya, I can tell you, these men don't worry about money. None of them. They're sincere when they tell you money isn't an issue. It was very hard for me to learn to accept, too." Harmony looked at Roman, and Anya could feel the love radiate between the two of them. "They have hard jobs. They're paid well and are, to a person, the best protectors, providers, and solace on the face of the earth."

Anya pulled her gaze from the couple across from her to Malice, who was staring down at her. "How did I ever get so lucky? How did I find you out of all the people in the world?" she whispered in Russian.

"You didn't find me. I found you," he replied in the same low voice. "And I would have kept searching for you if I missed you in Russia. I believe you've been my destiny since time began."

Anya sighed and blinked back the tears welling in her eyes. The waiter arrived before she could say anything, but she prayed her eyes told the man beside her how she felt. Her world had tied itself around him. She was a part of his world, no longer joined to her past. Her future was big, bright, and more than a little intimidating, but she could do anything with Malice beside her.

* * *

"COULD you hold him while I try these on?" Harmony handed Carter to her. Anya took the baby and cuddled him into her arms. She spoke in Russian to the little guy, saying, "You are handsome, are you not? Yes, you are." A shiver of realization ran across her skin, and she jerked her head up, looking for what had caused it.

Malice was across the store, and he was staring at her. She smiled at him and rocked the baby in her arms. A slow smile spread across his face, and he walked in her direction. "How did you end up with the baby?"

"Maggie wanted to sit down, so Roman took her and Iris to the inside area. I think he called it the … mall?" She shrugged. "Harmony wanted to try on a dress. I am holding him. He is beautiful, is he not?"

"He is." Malice dropped his arm over her shoulders. "Have you ever thought about having children?"

Anya glanced up at him. "What girl does not? I worry I would not be a good mother, you know? Would I know what to do?"

Malice smiled down at her. "Parenting is a lot of guesswork. If you love your children and make sure they're safe and cared for, you're already a good parent."

"I think that would be true," Anya said as she looked down at the little boy. "Thank you for the clothes. You bought me too many."

Malice laughed. "No, I didn't. I have a friend you'll meet. Her name is Val. She has more clothes than this department store."

Anya frowned and looked across the expanse of the store. "Is that not wasteful?"

Malice drew a deep breath and made a wavering motion with his head. "In her case, no. I'll explain sometime when I'm able."

"I will remind you of this." She was intrigued by how someone could have and wear so many clothes.

"When will we leave for Virginia?" She rocked the baby, who was sleeping peacefully in her arms.

"I don't think Lilly will have a problem clearing you from PT. So, probably Tuesday."

"How will we go? Driving? Will you go back to work? What will I do?" She inhaled sharply. "Sorry. I am …" She slipped into Russian. "I am working these questions in my head. They do not stop. Always going around and around."

He dropped his hand to her hip. "Instead of chasing them around, ask me. If I can answer them, I will. So, we'll fly to Washington, DC, and I'll ask H to pick us up. We'll go to my house in Virginia. No, I'm not on deck for a mission, but that isn't always a guarantee. Something could come up. I have friends in the area who would be happy to help out if I do have to leave. As far as what you do, that's up to you. What do you want to do?"

"I cannot make a living teaching how to fire weapons, so … I do not know. Maybe go to classes? Maybe learn to read English better." She shrugged and looked down at the baby in her arms.

Malice cleared his throat. "You know what?

You *can* make a living teaching people how to shoot weapons."

She jerked her head up. "How?"

"We have what are called shooting ranges. People pay for private instruction. People would pay through the nose to learn how to fire a rifle as well as you do."

"Through the nose?" Anya shivered a bit. "That is distasteful."

Malice chuckled. "It means they would pay a lot of money."

"Oh." Anya made a face at him. "Still distasteful."

"I never really thought of it, but you're right."

"I'm back," Harmony said as she approached. "Is he still asleep?"

"He is," Malice said. "He's a good sleeper."

Harmony made a motion to take the baby. "Both my babies are. Anya, are you done?"

"A long time ago," Anya said as she gave Carter back to his mom. "He has purchased too much."

Harmony chuckled. "You're lucky you're a perfect size four. I'm an eleven who should be a ten but is more comfortable in a twelve. Someday, I may get my pre-baby body back."

"I hope not. You're sexy as hell just the way you are," Roman said from behind her.

Harmony squeaked and jumped around. "I told you to not sneak up on me like that. Lord above."

Anya leaned into Malice as they made their way out of the store. Happiness like she'd never felt before floated around and carried her. She closed her eyes for a second as they walked and sent a message to her babushka. "I am happy." She smiled and took a deep breath. For the first time in her life, she had no worries.

CHAPTER 23

*A*nya woke and stretched slowly, opening her eyes. The sun-drenched room had a view of the apple orchard in the backyard. Anya sat up and blinked a couple of times, trying to focus on the clock on the other side of the room.

She didn't often take naps, but the past weekend, she and Malice consummated every room in his massive house. Sex with that man was magnificent. Her body ached in the best possible way.

The cell phone Malice gave her vibrated in her pocket.

She smiled at his picture when she pulled it out. She swiped the face and said, "You love me."

"I do," he agreed. "I'm going to swing by my friend Flack's house. Val and Smith just got back from an assignment, so I thought I'd invite all of them over tonight. We can order pizza and visit."

"This is the woman with the clothes?"

"Yep. Her husband is Russian."

Anya blinked at that bit of information. "And he was on an assignment?"

"A long story, and a lot of it is classified," Malice apologized.

"That is no problem." She meant that. She was happy to be an American; if he could never tell her everything involving his work, she would accept it and be grateful. "No fruit on the pizza." She shivered. H had ordered a pizza with fruit on it the first night they were home. It was disgusting. "I did not like it."

"I got that message loud and clear. Did you get a chance to rest today?"

"I just woke up from a nap." She pushed her hair off her shoulder. "I am a lady of luxury. I will get soft."

"I like you soft," Malice growled into the phone.

"You like it better when I can keep up with you. Yes?" They'd become increasingly athletic during their couplings. It was something they both enjoyed.

"Oh, fuck. Woman, you kill me."

"No, you, I will not kill," she purred. "I will make you scream my name, though."

"Damn it. Now I have to sit outside Flack's house for a minute to control myself."

"Then my work is done." Anya laughed and caught a reflection of light against the wall. She turned around to see what the sun was reflecting against.

"I'll see you in about ten or twenty minutes. I love you."

"I love you, too." She hung up and twisted around. Where had that reflection come from? She walked from room to room. The colonial house was massive and very luxurious. Anya walked across the large open foyer to the kitchen area after finding nothing that would have caused the reflection she saw in the sunroom. She pushed the door to the kitchen open.

The blow to her head sent bolts of pain through her brain, dropping her to the floor. She rolled onto her back and looked up. *Karl.*

Anya woke up as her wrists were cinched painfully behind her back. "You were hard to track down, my little whore." Karl held a knife in his hand and placed it under her chin, forcing her to lift her head.

"Why are you here? Why are you looking for me?" Anya swallowed hard, and she felt the knife pierce her skin. Karl's eyes went to the trickle of blood she felt slowly trail down her neck. Anya used the time to look for others. She recognized Gusev and another lieutenant behind him. There were three others that she could see. At least six. How could she warn Malice?

Karl lifted his eyes to hers. "You told the Americans. For this, I will cut off your skin, piece by piece. I will listen to you scream and let you putrefy in your own fluids. When you think you are going insane with pain, I will make you suffer more. You will not die fast or easy. That conquest would have ensured my status as the premier military authority in Russia."

"I do not know what you're talking about."

As he stared at her, a sneer slowly spread across his face. "Dima knew. He told you."

"I can swear Dima told me nothing, but you would not listen to what I have to say. These hired cock suckers have fed you lies. Everyone in the camp knows Gusev would do anything to advance."

"Your rifle killed our men," Gusev said.

"Because they turned on your father!" Anya's

brain was scrambling, but she concentrated on keeping her eyes leveled and staring at Karl. She had to delay the execution. Because there was no doubt that was why he was there; he was going to kill her. She could see it in his eyes. "The American came too late. Your father's men killed him."

"Liar!" Gusev screamed at her.

Karl held up a hand, stilling his lieutenant. "Why are you with the American?" His knife's pressure lessened slightly.

Anya shrugged as best as she could with her hands bound and a knife under her chin. "Look at this place. Look at where you are. Can you blame me? He keeps me here for the sex. It is better than Siberia." Karl's eyes traveled around the room as if seeing it for the first time.

Anya's phone rang, skittering along the hard-wood floor. She sighed heavily. "He checks up on me. He does not trust me. He will come straight home if I don't answer it."

Karl directed one of the men to get the phone. "Put it on speaker," he demanded and lifted the knife, pressing it harder into the vulnerable flesh behind her chin. "Be very careful, whore."

"Da," she answered in Russian when Gusev answered the call and held it up to her face.

"Hey, I was only able to order pizza with fruit." There was laughter in his voice.

Anya looked into Karl's eyes as she spoke. "You know I like fruit on my pizza. This is good. Are you still coming home in six hours?"

Malice was silent for a minute, and then the laughter was back in his voice. "What? Oh yeah, six hours at least. It could be more."

"Yes, at least," Anya said. "I am tired. Do not call again, yes? I will take a nap."

"No problem. Sleep well."

"Goodbye." Anya prayed it wouldn't be the last time she said those words. The connection ended.

"So, for the next six hours, you are mine." Karl's sneer reappeared. "There are no neighbors to hear your screams." He removed the knife, walked back to the kitchen island, and leaned against it, staring at her. She waited. It was Karl's move in their game of life or death.

Anya's eyes flicked to the camera mounted in the corner of the room. The sensor above it flashed red. Karl saw the direction of her gaze and turned, but the light had gone dark. "The cameras and the alarm have been neutralized."

Anya returned her stare to the man in front of her. "By who? Gusev? He is an idiot." Which was

God's honest truth. The man used others and took credit for their work.

"Please let me kill her," Gusev growled from where he stood beside Karl. Anya didn't alter her gaze. She stared straight into Karl's eyes.

"Go to the van. I want my kit." Karl sneered at the man. He walked back to her and stared at her momentarily before turning. She wasn't expecting the flying fist as he spun back in her direction. Pain exploded across her cheek, and she fell from the stool where she'd been sitting. Her shoulder crashed into the hardwood floor, and Anya gasped in pain as her head hit the floor next. The bottom of Gusev's boot was the last thing she saw before her vision exploded in a mushroom of red.

* * *

MALICE BOLTED from Flack's kitchen. "She's in trouble. Six people, my address!"

Val, Smith, and Flack ran with him. "Six perps at your residence," Addy called after them as she grabbed up Brooke. "I'll call CCS."

Malice didn't answer, but Smith grabbed his shoulder as he opened the door to his car. "We need a plan. If you run in without one, she could be killed."

"There's an orchard behind the house. My root cellar has a hidden tunnel to the house," Malice said. "Get in. We can devise a plan on the way."

The four of them jumped into his SUV, and Malice pulled out of the driveway, going way too fast. "Where does the tunnel enter the house?"

"The basement." Malice slammed on the brakes and swerved around a kid on a bike that shot out of a driveway.

"Slow down," Flack said calmly. "We need to make it to your place. We're only a few minutes away."

"Drop me and Smith at the front. We'll move up the driveway. Text us when you're in the house and ready to enter. I'll come in the front. Smith will take the back." Val pulled her automatic from her purse.

Flack put his phone on speaker. "Go."

"She's alive but tied up. I found her in the kitchen. There were four armed men I could see. I didn't leave the camera on. I'll try to grab pictures, but they'll move or kill her if they see me monitoring them," the woman in CCS said. "Whoever tried to bypass the system was an amateur and fucked it up. The audio alarm and reporting are bypassed, but that's it."

Malice turned the corner and accelerated. Hang on, baby. "Facial rec?"

"Working it."

"Who the fuck would be after her?"

Malice ground out the name of the only bastard who would be searching for her. "Karl Rostova."

"I'll compare with that name," CCS said.

"How would he know to come here?" Val asked from the back seat. "Slow the fuck down, Mal. You don't want neighbors calling the cops."

Malice let off the accelerator. They were at least five minutes away. "I put my fucking address down on the hospital admission paperwork in Alaska. *Fuck!*" He slammed his fist against the steering wheel.

"Confirmed identification on Karl Rostova. Fury, Alpha, and Archangel are coming online in three, two, one …"

"Sitrep." Archangel's voice boomed over the connection.

Malice snapped, "Karl Rostova is holding Anya at my residence."

"How in the hell—" Fury started but was interrupted by CCS. "I can confirm the hospital in

Nome was hacked, and admission records were downloaded."

"I used my address. I had no idea Karl was after her at that point. I'm responsible." Fuck, if that bastard hurt her, he'd never forgive himself.

"Save the pity party for later," Fury interjected. "Do you have a plan?"

"Yes," Malice snapped back at the bastard.

"Then execute it," Archangel said. "These are known terrorists on American soil, and as war criminals, they don't have legal standing. Do what you need to do. CCS, patch me through to the Virginia attorney general."

"On it."

Malice slowed down just before his driveway, and Val and Smith exited the vehicle. He drove by the long, winding driveway at a normal speed before stepping on the gas again. He pulled off at the orchard, put the SUV into Park, and turned it off. He and Flack were out of the vehicle a second later. Flack kept pace with him as he sprinted through the apple trees. He made it to the old root cellar and opened the door. Flack was down the stairs, and he followed. At the back of the small earthen cave, Mal pulled a wooden shelving unit, and it moved, showing a tunnel.

"This tunnel is from the Prohibition?" Flack asked.

"Yeah. They stored the alcohol out here in the middle of the orchard." It was one of the biggest selling points of the house for him. An emergency egress if he needed it. He turned on the flashlight on his cell phone, and they ran, stooped over, through the musty tunnel to the door that ended at his home. Mal keyed in a code, and the locks popped. He winced at the sound.

"Fuck, that was loud," Flack said.

He nodded but pushed open the door. Anya's scream was the first thing that registered as the door swung into the house. Malice bolted for the door, but Flack practically tackled him to stop him. "We've got to let Smith and Val know."

Malice shrugged off Flack and growled, "Then do it now." He bounded up the steps two at a time as Flack cussed and flew up after him.

Malice hesitated at the top of the stairs as he eased the door open. Flack's hand landed on his shoulder. "I'm sending the text. We count to ten, then we go."

Anya's scream tore through the house, and Malice was gone. He charged at a dead run through the house.

The door to the kitchen opened, and Malice fired. He jumped and pushed the body he'd just shot, slamming against the swinging door. His weapon was up, and he fired at the man in front of Anya, who was alive. *Thank God.*

Flack's weapon fired, as did his. Men in the kitchen dropped like swatted flies. "Behind the counter by the oven!" Anya screamed, and Malice flew across the kitchen, slid over the granite-covered island, and landed facing a cowering Karl Rostova.

There was no holding back. Malice grabbed the man by the neck and lifted him from his crouched position. His hands slapped at Malice's. Malice locked stares with the man and pushed him, pinning his back on top of the granite. Spittle foamed at the corners of Rostova's mouth. He tried to speak but had no air and no way of getting it. Rostova's face turned a brilliant red, and his eyes bulged as Malice tightened his grip. "You signed your death warrant coming after my woman." Malice noticed when Rostova tried to go for his weapon. He tightened his grip and felt cartilage under his fingers break. Gunshots popped outside the kitchen, but Malice didn't divert his attention. He could hear Flack talking to Anya, but even that didn't pull his attention away from the man he was killing.

Mal lowered his face to Rostova's and smiled evilly. "Do you know who I am? I am all the rage you've ever felt. I am the embodiment of the world's hatred. I am death, and I am sending you to hell. Never forget my face because I will hunt you through eternity." He tightened his grip and watched as the life drained out of the man. When Rostova's eyes fixated, Mal released his grip and snapped his head toward where Anya had been seated.

Val was helping Flack untie her, but Anya wasn't looking at the people who were freeing her. She was staring at Smith.

Malice jogged over and dropped to his knees in front of her. He looked down at her foot. "Oh, fuck, babe. What did they do?" Blood covered the top of her foot.

Anya's hand fell on his shoulder. He gazed up at her. "Toenails. I will be fine."

Val shook her head. "Fucking bastards. Smith, ask CCS to have a Mercy team come out?"

Smith's low voice immediately spoke, but Malice leaned over and grabbed a hand towel off the counter. He carefully lifted her foot and wrapped it in the terry cloth, being careful to not put any weight on the two nailbeds that had no protection. He tucked the fabric around her ankle to secure it and stood, picking her up. "I'll take you to the bedroom."

"Wait, wait. This man." She pointed to Smith, who had just finished talking to CCS. "This man, who is he?"

Val frowned. "My husband. Smithson Young."

Anya shook her head, and in Russian, she said, "He is Abrasha Molchalin. Younger, yes, but he could be the image of the man."

Malice cradled her in his arms. He glanced over at Smith. "As in the oligarch who funded the Switzerland invasion?"

"Yes." Anya winced and lifted her hand to her cheek, which had a bruise the size of an orange forming on it. "I have been hit in the head, but I swear he is a duplicate. He could pass for Abrasha. I know this."

Flack stepped over the dead body at the door. "The exterior is clear. Their vehicle, a ten-passenger van, is out front. Dom Ops and the coroner are en route. We have the lead on the investigations, thanks to Archangel. Smith, you and Val, get out of here. I know the investigators through Addy. Mal's SUV is at the back of the orchard. Use the tunnel downstairs to get to the root cellar. You can walk to it from there."

The big man nodded and extended his hand to Val. "I'll be back and introduce myself properly later," Val said as Smith ushered her out of the kitchen. Flack followed them out.

Anya dropped her head onto his chest. "Thank God, you understood me."

"I did. It was my fault he found you. I used this address when I checked you into the hospital. They hacked that system. They must have been waiting for us."

"Karl said they had been. He flew to Canada and came across the border." Anya lifted her foot. The blood hadn't soaked through the thick cloth yet. "Gusev wanted to chop off my toes. Karl told him to pull the toenails so I wouldn't bleed out. He thought he had six hours. If he did not, I would be dead. The bastard was getting something to eat when you came in."

Malice walked over to the dead body holding the kitchen door open and headed to the bedroom. Flack put his hand to the phone as they passed him, covering the mic. "We have a Mercy team en route. ETA thirty minutes. I'll handle identifying and getting rid of the trash. Val and Smith took out two at the front and back of the residence. A total of ten."

"I'll come out when the Mercy team gets here." Mal continued his stride toward the main bedroom.

"I will be okay." Anya wiped at her tear-stained face. "Maybe no shoes for a time."

Malice huffed out a noise he hoped sounded like amusement, but there was nothing funny about the situation. He laid her down on the bed and dropped to his knee beside her. "I heard you screaming. I … God, I lost it. I fucking lost it." His heart had stopped. He lost all sense of mission and training. He just knew he had to get to her. Had to stop those bastards from hurting her.

Anya placed her hand on his cheek. "This is not your fault. This is Karl. Karl was sick." She touched her head. "Here. Very sick. He liked to watch people in pain. He liked to cause the pain."

"But if I hadn't—"

Anya shook her head and spoke in Russian, "If the moon was purple if the earth didn't spin, if, if, if …We cannot control the actions of others. We cannot. We can only control how we respond to them. Karl is dead. I heard you. I heard you curse him through eternity. I know you will protect me even when we are dust. This is truth. This is us. This is our love. We are each other's destiny."

Mal traced her cheek with his fingers. "Since the beginning of time, until the last star fades in the heavens, I'm yours, and you're mine. We are each other's destiny."

CHAPTER 24

our Months Later:

Mal woke as soon as Anya ducked under the covers. She kissed her way down his chest, and his cock went from sleep to diamond hard so fast that if he were standing, he probably would have passed out because of how fast his blood rushed south. His hands found her hair, and he tangled them up in that beautiful fall of blonde.

"Good morning." He hissed the last syllable of the greeting when she took the top of his shaft into her mouth. The woman laughed, and the vibration damn near made his eyes do a three-sixty in their sockets. Her hand cupped his balls, and she lowered, taking his shaft into her mouth. The head of his cock bumped the back of her throat. "Fuck."

His knees lifted, and his hands tightened without intent in her hair. She lifted and licked the crown of his shaft like a fucking lollipop and then dropped down again.

Fuck, he was going to cum if she didn't slow down. As much as he was enjoying it … He lifted and grabbed her, popping her off his cock. She wrapped her arms around his neck and squirmed up his lap. He used one hand to center under her core, and she sat down on his cock. The evil little nymph arched backward and planted her hands just above his knees. His hand followed the arch of that beautiful body between her breasts to her neck. She lifted and dropped down. He moaned at the same time she did. Mal arched backward, too, and braced both arms behind him. He waited as she moved a bit, then thrust his hips. Fuck, Anya was so bendy that that position had instantly become a favorite. He closed his eyes and felt the sweep of her long blonde hair against his legs. Her core's slight resistance as he entered and withdrew was unbelievably amplified by the arch of her back.

Sweat formed as they made love. He straightened and grabbed her hips. Carefully, he untangled them and dropped her to her back. He pulled one of her legs up to his hip and thrust inside her again. Anya's hands found his shoulders, and her nails bit into his skin. That bite of pain launched them into a frenzied dash to their climax. Mal felt her tighten and then snap. Anya's vocal, panted sound of release was the absolute limit of his endurance. He flicked his hips twice before he emptied inside her.

Mal caught himself on his arm and tried to catch his breath. "Woman, you are going to kill me."

Anya moved her head from left to right and back again before she said in a breathless voice, "No. Never kill you."

Mal glanced over at the clock. "We have to get ready soon."

"Why would someone have a wedding at ten in the morning?" Anya opened an eye and turned her head to the clock. "Especially after a late-night party the night before?"

"H has to catch a plane back to Europe." Mal dropped to his side and wiped the sweat from his brow. "We can come home and sleep after the lunch thing."

"That lunch thing took Londyn a month to get

ready for." Anya propped herself up on her elbow. "She used a couple of my recipes. Did I tell you?"

Mal reached up and pushed her hair back over her shoulder. The scar from the knife wound was purple against her skin, but he didn't notice it anymore. It was just a part of the woman he loved. "You did. I want to try them. Do you regret getting married at the Justice of the Peace?"

Anya held up her hand and smiled at the thick gold band. "No. I do not. Londyn wants the white gown and celebration. I want you. That is all. I didn't want to take the attention off Londyn, but I did not want to wait, either. This is best." Anya leaned over, kissed him, then dropped onto his chest, draping over him. "Do you regret the haste?"

"Not at all. We'll get shit about it when people figure out we got married without them being there."

Anya snorted. "This we can fix. We will have a party here when all the celebrations for Ice and Londyn are done."

"That's true." Malice ran his hand through her hair. "What time did Val want you to come over?"

"She said the wedding was all set up in their backyard and to come over about two hours before, so eight." Mal glanced at the clock again. It was only six, so they could be lazy.

"All of us are going to get our makeup and hair done. Is this normal?" Anya lifted up to look at him.

She was absolutely beautiful without makeup, and he couldn't imagine her hair other than the way she wore it. Either in a ponytail or falling straight past her shoulders. "I think for weddings, yes. For Val, every day." Mal rolled his eyes.

"She says I will become addicted to makeup." Anya made a face. "I don't think so."

"You're beautiful without makeup."

"You are biased." She said biased in Russian. Their conversations were often a mix of English and Russian.

"I am." He wouldn't deny it. "Oh, I have a present for you." He rolled over and grabbed an envelope from the nightstand.

"What is this?" She looked at the envelope like it was poisonous when he handed it to her.

"Remember the shooting range I took you to a couple of months ago?" Malice sat up, and so did Anya. She narrowed her eyes and stared at him. "I do."

"Well, I bought it." Malice felt heat run to his

cheeks. Fuck, he was blushing again. Only with her.

Her mouth dropped open, and she asked in Russian, "What does that mean? Tell me because I am sure I misunderstood your English."

"You want to make money, true?" he asked her.

"This is true. I don't like not having my own money," she admitted. It was something she felt strongly about, and he'd finally figured out a way she could provide that income for herself.

"I bought this range, but you will be the manager. You will pay yourself and the employees, and each month you make a profit, that profit will go toward you buying the range from me. You'll own it outright eventually."

As she stared at him, a smile spread across her face. "You knew I wouldn't take it from you as a present."

Mal nodded. "I knew. I knew you would want to purchase it, and I figured out how I could make that happen."

She held the envelope to her breast. "You understand." The love in his wife's eyes was something he'd never get tired of seeing.

"I'm learning to understand."

"Six times out of ten?" She laughed.

He shook his head. "Seven times out of ten."

She made a face, contemplating his words. "Okay, seven times out of ten." She pounced on him and pushed him back into the mattress. "I love you."

He wrapped her in his arms and rolled on top of her. "I love you, too." He lowered for a kiss and thanked destiny for his woman. He had a perfect family, not by blood, but by friendship and now by love and a golden ring on her finger. It had taken over thirty years, but Malice had finally found where he belonged—with Anya.

H stared out of the taxi taking him to his Paris apartment. He'd tried to duck out of the wedding, booking a plane the same day, but Ice, the fucker, had changed the time of the wedding so he could attend.

Ice knew what he was going through. He understood the pain H was feeling, but Ice had also pulled out his fucking degree and worked with him to get over the damage Ysabel had caused.

It had helped, but ... The ache in his gut watching his friends marry was strong, it was vivid, and it burned like acid being poured on his skin. It could have been him standing at the front of the aisle. It could have been Ysabel walking toward him, but she'd handed him his ring, told him she didn't love him, and left him standing in the middle of a crowded ballroom filled with Europe's wealthiest families.

When he tried to follow her, her father's bodyguards blocked his way. Ysabel didn't look back. H tried everything he knew to contact her, but every avenue was closed. She left a voice mail on his phone. He glanced at the icon for that voice mail. He knew the words by heart. "Stop trying to contact me. I don't want to hear from you again. Leave me alone. We are done. Don't be pathetic."

Pathetic. H drew a deep breath and hit the delete button. Ysabel was right. He was being pathetic. The relationship had lasted over a year. He'd asked her to marry him, and she'd agreed. Something had happened in the week that he'd left to complete a mission. But what?

H paid the driver and made his way inside his apartment building. He walked up the four flights of stairs and let himself into his apartment. After showering, he made his way into the kitchen to open a bottle of wine.

A knock on his door spun him from the counter. He opened a cabinet and pulled an automatic off the top shelf. He pulled back the slide to ensure a bullet was lodged in the chamber and made his way to the front door. H glanced out the peephole and frowned. He opened the door, his weapon shielded from view.

"You must help me." Ysabel's father had aged ten years in the eight months he'd been gone. "He has Ysabel, and he will kill her."

Ice-cold rage cinched Harbinger's gut. "Who?"

"Abrasha Molchalin."

WANT to read Harbinger's story? Click here!

ALSO BY KRIS MICHAELS

Kings of the Guardian Series

Jacob: Kings of the Guardian Book 1

Joseph: Kings of the Guardian Book 2

Adam: Kings of the Guardian Book 3

Jason: Kings of the Guardian Book 4

Jared: Kings of the Guardian Book 5

Jasmine: Kings of the Guardian Book 6

Chief: The Kings of Guardian Book 7

Jewell: Kings of the Guardian Book 8

Jade: Kings of the Guardian Book 9

Justin: Kings of the Guardian Book 10

Christmas with the Kings

Drake: Kings of the Guardian Book 11

Dixon: Kings of the Guardian Book 12

Passages: The Kings of Guardian Book 13

Promises: The Kings of Guardian Book 14

The Siege: Book One, The Kings of Guardian Book 15

The Siege: Book Two, The Kings of Guardian Book 16

A Backwater Blessing: A Kings of Guardian Crossover Novella

Montana Guardian: A Kings of Guardian Novella

Guardian Defenders Series

Gabriel

Maliki

John

Jeremiah

Frank

Creed

Sage

Bear

Billy

Guardian Security Shadow World

Anubis (Guardian Shadow World Book 1)

Asp (Guardian Shadow World Book 2)

Lycos (Guardian Shadow World Book 3)

Thanatos (Guardian Shadow World Book 4)

Tempest (Guardian Shadow World Book 5)

Smoke (Guardian Shadow World Book 6)

Reaper (Guardian Shadow World Book 7)

Phoenix (Guardian Shadow World Book 8)

Valkyrie (Guardian Shadow World Book 9)

Flack (Guardian Shadow World Book 10)

Ice (Guardian Shadow World Book 11)

Malice (Guardian Shadow World Book 12)

Harbinger (Guardian Shadow World Book 13)

Centurion (Guardian Shadow World Book 14)

Hollister (A Guardian Crossover Series)

Andrew (Hollister-Book 1)

Zeke (Hollister-Book 2)

Declan (Hollister- Book 3)

Ken (Hollister - Book 4)

Barry (Hollister - Book 5)

Hope City

Hope City - Brock

HOPE CITY - Brody- Book 3

Hope City - Ryker - Book 5

Hope City - Killian - Book 8

Hope City - Blayze - Book 10

The Long Road Home

Season One:

My Heart's Home

Season Two:

Searching for Home (A Hollister-Guardian Crossover Novel)

Season Three:

A Home for Love (A Hollister Crossover Novel)

STAND-ALONE NOVELS

A Heart's Desire - Stand Alone

Hot SEAL, Single Malt (SEALs in Paradise)

Hot SEAL, Savannah Nights (SEALs in Paradise)

Hot SEAL, Silent Knight (SEALs in Paradise)

Join my newsletter for fun updates and release information!

>>>Kris' Newsletter<<<

ABOUT THE AUTHOR

Wall Street Journal and USA Today Bestselling Author, Kris Michaels is the alter ego of a happily married wife and mother. She writes romance, usually with characters from military and law enforcement backgrounds.

Printed in Great Britain
by Amazon

44813920R00169